INDUCTION

To Sarah,
All the best!

David Brush

To those I've loved and those I've hated, in equal parts.

CHAPTER ONE

The young man floated through the void, surrounded by darkness. Off in the distance, he could just make out a tiny speck of light, nearly buried in the thick, black sea. He swam towards it with all his might, longing for its warmth, longing for its energy. As he neared the whipping flames, he finally realized their source.

"Haley," called the boy through the blank space.

No response. The girl's hair continued to swirl up into a blinding inferno.

"Haley," he said again, reaching for her shoulder. As he touched her, she turned to face him at last, her emerald eyes flickering beneath the dancing fire.

"Never again," said the girl, reaching out and tapping him on the forehead. "Never again."

He closed his eyes as he felt the chemicals begin to warp his perception. He screamed out, but the emptiness swallowed it whole. When at last he opened his eyes again, the girl's face had already begun to disintegrate. Her skin slopped off, melting her features together into one long river of flesh. Horrified, the boy turned away from her, toward the mirror suspended behind him. He looked into the reflection at his hazel eyes, covered in a thick layer of glaze. This time he didn't scream, he just closed his eyes again and fell...

James Mercer shot upright in his bed sometime around four a.m. His eyes jolted around his room until he realized that he had been dreaming again, the same dream for nearly twelve months now. He lay back down against the sweat-soaked pillow and stared up at the ceiling until dawn broke. Giving up on anymore sleep, he rolled out of bed to start the new day. The haze of exhaustion plagued his every action as he dressed himself, showered quickly, and poured a mug full of coffee down his throat to help pull his mind back into something resembling human cognition. It helped, but the fog lingered, resting just below the surface of the caffeine high. James scooped his backpack up off of the kitchen floor and made his way out of the small apartment he shared with his father.

The sun had risen well above the horizon by the time he made it to the lab he worked in. The facility was one of a dozen situated in the big, bland building that sat inconspicuously in the center of Dunton. While it wasn't as grand as some of the major Neuro Corporation complexes, the smaller offshoot was as well-equipped as any other. Walking down the wide hall towards his office, the boy noticed one of the new "unity" posters projected across the wall. On it, a chemist stood proudly against the rising sun, holding a flask out towards the new day, with the inscription NEURO CORPORATION: THROUGH CHEMISTRY, PEACE plastered around the centered art. He shook his head as he continued on down the hall.

James keyed his way into the lab and greeted Dr. Omar Karich with a nod. The older chemist was already hovering near the lone solvent sink in the room, pouring acetone into the glassware that they would be using shortly. Nearby, hands fidgeting under the downturned panel of the old fume hood that adorned the lab, stood Haley Hall, preparing a variety of stock solutions for the coming day. She brushed a strand of her auburn hair out of her face and smiled at James as he walked in.

"You're late," said Dr. Karich, drawing him back to reality.

"Sorry," mumbled James, as he tossed his backpack down at his work bench. "I lost track of time again."

"You're lucky you're not easily replaced," said the doctor with a smile. "If I hadn't spent the last four years turning you into an actual chemist, I'd just go grab someone new off the street and be done with it. You're not so young anymore after all."

James grinned. "What can I say, old age has left me jaded."

"Well, jaded or not, I need you at your best today. We have a lot of work to do and not a lot of time left to do it. The Committee on the Progression of Scientific Inquiry wants a full report on our work by next Tuesday. Apparently they're getting antsy waiting for us to finish up."

"We've created the first synthetic human cell capable of utilizing photosynthesis. It's one of the big milestones of the IMMORTAL Initiative. I'm surprised they're trying to rush us; we're way ahead of schedule."

"The government needs their victories where they can get them. Our work will be a welcome distraction for them to parade around. Besides, the IMMORTAL Initiative is Dr. Nightrick's own pet project. I'm not surprised that they're trying to turn up some good news for him. After that disaster at the Valker Plant, he'll need all the good news he can get. Anyway, whenever you have a minute, I'd like a quick word with you in private."

"Now is fine," said James, walking into the office that sat adjacent to the lab without waiting for a response. He looked around the small room, littered with old books and scraps of paper with all manner of notes scribbled onto them. A small desk lamp cast a dull yellow light into the otherwise dark space. Dr. Karich walked in behind him and circled the cluttered desk.

"Don't you think you deserve better than a broom closet?" said James. "You're one of the best chemists in the entire country. Why do you let Neuro Corporation treat you like a pauper?"

Dr. Karich shrugged. "As long as they keep financing our work, I couldn't care less what kind of office they give me. Government funds are a little scarce right now; we're lucky we have what we have. I didn't ask you to join me in here to discuss the size of my office. I wanted to talk to you about the next few weeks," said the doctor, signaling for the boy to take a seat. "Your birthday is approaching."

James nodded, easing himself into one of the patchy, leather chairs that sat adjacent to the wide desk. "I won't be the same after the procedure. I'll just be another mindless cog in the slave machine Nightrick is building."

"Induction isn't so bad," said Dr. Karich, sitting down across from him. "You don't lose as much of your personality as some of the dissidents like to drone on about. From what I understand of it, it's as simple as falling in love."

"Oh, it's not so bad? That's easy for you to say though, isn't it? After all, your generation got a pass on it."

"Well it'd be wasteful to Induct people who have left behind their reproductive years. Listen, don't misunderstand what I'm saying here, James, I agree with you. The procedure shouldn't be mandatory. However, with Dr. Nightrick as this country's de facto ruler now, you have to understand that a lot of things are going to change. The Raynon Uprising burned the old world to the ground and left a new one resting in its ashes."

James frowned. "Last time I checked, we still vote for our leaders."

"Sure, and every cycle they slither off to the capital to act like they have any power left, but everyone knows that they signed it away to bring peace back to the Earth a decade ago. We nearly entered the Stone Age again, James, you're too young to remember what it was like. Every day we'd wake up and wonder when the next atomic weapon would detonate or when the next band of rebels would ride into the city to slaughter whomever they deemed to be their enemies on that given day. Neighbors turned against neighbors, brothers killed brothers, and all in the name of survival. As a species, we fully reverted back into our primal form. Sacrifices had to be made."

"Don't lecture me on sacrifice," said James, subconsciously tearing at the frayed leather with his fingers. "I lost as much as everyone else did. And why? Because our ape species couldn't stand the idea that we weren't alone in the universe. One arrogant worldview traded for another, I suppose."

Dr. Karich leaned back in his chair ever so slightly. "While the discovery of alien life was in fact what triggered the panic, it wasn't the reason that the world burned. Hell, all we found were single-celled organisms. It wasn't that earth-shattering really, almost everyone had expected it to come at some point or another. The reason we nearly lost everything is because humans, in general, are easy to scare. Fear is the lord of all violence, and its dominion knows no bounds among men. Once you work an idiot up to a fever pitch, the only way to stop them is with force. You can't reason with a fool, that's the unfortunate symptom of being one. The riots started because of the discovery, sure, but it was the unfounded fear of a pandemic that triggered the war. Though I think his methods were barbaric, Nightrick quelled the Uprising and returned us to peace. He saved humanity from itself, and if I had to guess, that's why Induction exists in the first place. He means to breed the stupid out of people."

"I think I'm going be sick. You're obviously blinded by your friendship with him. Look around you for a minute. Turn on the news and tell me what you see. This is peace? That's odd, because I could swear there was a war going on right now. I guess as long as we refrain from calling it that, it doesn't exist."

"It's not nearly the same scale as it was," replied the doctor, meeting the young man's gaze.

"Nightrick has lost damn near half the country. What do you think will happen when the rebels finally get a foothold on the capital? They'll probably start to purge everyone who's remained loyal to the regime, and that obviously includes the Inducted. One way or another, after those chemicals enter my brain, my life is over."

"Don't be so dramatic, James, your life is just beginning. I called you in here because I want to talk to you about your future, not just the next few weeks. Your life will change after the procedure, but it won't be as bad as you think it will be. We're finally in range of succeeding. Soon, hunger will be a thing of the past, and no man, woman, or child will be left groveling for sustenance. We're going to give humanity a great gift. You and Haley have surpassed my wildest expectations, and I can safely say that without you two, this work would never have come to fruition. That's why I've put in to have both of you promoted. You'll be made doctors of science and given your own labs to run here at Neuro Corporation. There's not much else I can teach you. It's time you ventured out on your own."

James felt the blood rush out of his head. "I... I don't know what to say."

"Just promise me that you'll avoid doing anything stupid before your birthday. You'll do great things in your life, James. Don't let a moment of impulsiveness cost you your future."

As the sun began its slow retreat into the west, James and Haley made their way to one of the small restaurants that sat in the middle of downtown Dunton, just down the street from their laboratory. Tubes of neon light snaked all across the walls of the eatery in wild patterns, projecting their carefully choreographed displays out to the patrons enjoying their meals. The young couple sat in their usual booth against the wall, the one underneath the glowing guitar, and ate dinner as they always did, side by side, with the same light-hearted playfulness that had catalyzed their love in the first place.

"Not a lot of cars out tonight," said Haley, looking through the large window at the abandoned street. "I wonder what the hell is going on."

"It's the rally," replied James. "They've been plastering those propaganda posters all over the place. Nightrick is in town to commemorate the end of the Raynon Uprising."

"But why here? Dunton is a hole in the wall. He should've stayed in Dovaruss. Whenever he leaves the capital it means something is up."

James nodded. "Yup. We'll probably be under siege before the end of the month. His morale trips are having the opposite effect anymore. Whenever he shows up, it's like the kiss of death. If the rebels are trying to take Dunton, it'd be the closest the insurgency has gotten to Dovaruss in years."

She smiled at him. "Well maybe we should skip town."

"I wish," he said with a small frown.

"What's wrong?"

James sighed, avoiding eye contact with her as best he could. "We need to talk. My birthday is in six days. You know what they say, no drinks before eighteen and no dating past it."

"Before you say anything else, you know that I love you."

"I know...but we don't have a choice."

"You always have a choice. There's always an option. We could leave, like we talked about."

"To where?" he responded, still uncertain of how to proceed. "The Martian colonies? The Lunar? Unless you have a ship that we can use to break orbit, they'll find us. There's no place we could go that they wouldn't find us."

They sat in silence, neither meeting the other's gaze.

"I'll be right back, I'm going to take a leak," said James as he got up to leave. He made a beeline for the front register. After quickly paying, he walked towards the exit, causing the doors to slide away before him. As he stood there outside the restaurant in the cool air of fall at dusk, he felt a nagging guilt ensnare him.

"God dammit," he murmured, turning around and walking back into the restaurant. When he got to the table, he took Haley by the hand, and without another word they left.

The pair wandered aimlessly through the city as twilight burst forth in the sky above them. The glowing teal, blue, and purple coalesced so perfectly that for a moment, just a moment, the young couple forgot about the worries that plagued them. There was some comfort to be found in knowing that no matter what happened there on Earth, the entire universe that lay beyond it would carry on as if nothing had happened at all.

They walked along until a large, concrete barricade blocked them from continuing forward. Down the street, a large swarm of people had gathered around the amphitheater sitting in the middle of Kingswood Park.

"The rally," said Haley with a small scowl. "Guess we'll have to take the long way home."

"Or we could stay and watch," replied James, pointing towards the large building next to him. "I bet we could get a pretty good view of the stage from up there. I'd like to hear the sweet promises he makes us before we all get hammered for his fucking eugenics program."

"I don't know," she replied, eyeing the high rise. "His security is probably crawling all over the place."

"Oh come on," he said, taking her by the hand. "What's life without a little adventure?"

She walked along beside him, winding her fingers through his. "Fine, but let's try to avoid being detained."

He smiled at her. "In and out, I swear. Think you can reach that fire escape if I boost you up?"

"Let's find out."

With a heave, James raised her up, and she reached out, wrapping her hand around the metal grating of the staircase. She climbed onto the stairs, winding her leg through one of the steel bars and leaning back to help James up. He jumped, grabbing onto her extended arms. Straining, he pulled himself up. Once they were both firmly on the platform, they climbed along the building's exterior, stopping on the sixth floor.

Haley looked over the guardrail into the park below. The stage opened up directly in front of them. "I hate to admit it, but you were right. This is a hell of a view."

James nodded, pointing towards the podium. "And there's the man of the hour, Dr. Johnathan Nightrick, the great savior of Coren!"

Haley laughed, watching the procession below. All along the stage, large, glass shields rose up. Six black armored figures flanked their leader as he walked across the platform, fanning out behind the podium. The man who approached the microphone was tall, with a slim silhouette. His coat sat tight to his body, revealing an athletic physique. He cleared his throat, looking around at the crowd. "Citizens of Coren, my people, we gather here today in remembrance of the Raynon Uprising, and those who gave their lives that we might survive to honor theirs. Eleven years ago we faced our darkest hour. Our country withered in the face of a ruthless insurgency, our army stood tattered from years of endless war, and it looked as though the dawn we sought so desperately might never come. Well I'm here to tell you, today, despite what you've been told in the past, that dawn is still something we only dream towards. It's buried deep beneath the hour of the wolf, or wolves in our case. And make no mistake, those wolves are coming. They're coming to

Dunton, they're coming to Northgate, and they're coming to Dovaruss. Their hunger knows no bounds. They seek blood, and they'll devour us all, if we let them. To what end? What grand objective can they hope to accomplish by slaughtering their countrymen and burning their own cities? They believe that Induction is slavery. They believe that blood will break your chains. They cannot see the truth because they're blinded by self-righteousness. There are no chains. Induction is love, not bondage. It's chemistry, uniting well-paired couples in a perpetual state of adoration. It's progress, and it scares them because they know that they have no place in the coming world. Through eugenics, we'll create a better breed of person. We'll engineer and produce the specialists we need to finish ascending from this prison of rock that we've been confined to since time immemorial. This city will stand, as will all the others, because there's a truth that these terrorists do not understand. Bombs and bullets can never change the hearts and minds of the people. Only Induction can do that. Remember the words spoken..."

The thud against the glass was barely audible. Nightrick looked straight ahead as a large, spider web crack fanned out across the sheet, level with his forehead. He frowned, craning his head towards the apartments at the far end of the park before feeling the metal gauntlet on his shoulder pulling him down. The crowd roared in fury and fear, pressing towards the stage and away from it in a wave of flesh. The Shadow Guard circled the doctor, rushing him off the stage as another projectile slammed into the shielding, spreading the cracks even further.

From the balcony, James stared in amazement. "Holy shit."

The soldiers below looked up towards the building, spotting the young couple on the fire escape.

"Holy shit," said Haley, noticing the black clad men running towards the building. "Come on, quick."

They pushed the window open on the sixth floor and crawled into the building. There, on the floor, were two bodies that had been riddled with bullets. A wide pool of red connected the corpses.

"Oh my God..." started James as the door leading into the adjacent room shot open. Two black armored figures stepped through the opening, each cradling chrome coil rifles across their chests. The two soldiers regarded the couple for a moment.

"Please," said James, raising his hands. "You have to believe us; we had nothing to do with this."

"James?" said the heavier looking masked figure. "James Mercer?"

"Uhhh..."

The man removed his helmet. "Long time no see, bud."

"Matt? Oh my God, I'd heard you were dead!"

"Not dead." Matt laughed, pushing his hand through his thin, black hair. "Not quite yet anyway, but as you can see, I'm working on it. How're things going for you, buddy?"

"Is this really the best time for a reunion, Matt?" said his partner, turning towards him. "They're coming. Are you fucking stupid?"

"Shut it, Megan. I haven't seen this guy in ages. He's practically my brother. We grew up together here. I'm going to take a second to say hi."

"Well no need to do it here, you idiot. We can't let them go now anyway that you were brilliant enough to rip off your mask. We could've pinned the whole thing on them if you had half a brain in that head of yours."

"We're not framing my friend, and it's too late now anyway," said Matt, gesturing towards the staircase. "James, James's, I don't know, love interest? Stick close to us and you'll be just fine."

The group made their way out into the main hall of the floor, racing towards the staircase.

"We're going up," said Matt. "There's a helipad on the roof. We need to get the hell out of here before they get their own choppers into the air."

Two stories down, the rattle of boots against the stone floor reverberated off of the walls. As the fleeing group made it to the roof, Matt stopped for a moment to catch his breath, wheezing harder than the others. "Ok, load them up, Megan. It's time to go."

Megan turned towards James and Haley, pulling a smaller handgun out of her side holster. "Looks like you'll get to finish your little reunion back at base." She leveled her weapon and fired twice towards the couple. James pivoted in front of his girlfriend, taking both shots clean to the back and collapsing into her arms. Haley lifted him, but her world went dark the second Megan had lined up the next shot.

James lurched upright, his heart and mind racing. He looked around the cell that they'd been placed in. Beside him, Haley had been laid out on a red gel pad similar to the one he was sitting on. The steady rise and fall of her chest caused a small wave of relief to wash over him. Grey stone walls and very cheap looking aluminum furniture were the only other things to greet his gaze as he swiveled his head around the room. He could feel the dampness of a cold sweat leaking into his clothing as he strained to remember what had happened. All he could recall was the sound of the shot, crawling into the apartment, and then nothing. The sound of the metal door grating against its frame brought him back to reality. And then, as he watched Matt come trotting into the room, he remembered.

"You son of a bitch," he started in a fit of rage, pushing himself up off the ground.

"Calm down. Calmmmm down," said Matt, gesturing for James not to attack him. "My bad on all of this. Megan insisted that we couldn't leave you once I'd taken my helmet off and we had to get you here without you knowing where 'here' actually is. It'd be pretty hard to stay hidden for long if we took everyone we kidnapped through the front door."

"What are you going to do with us?" James replied, still weighing the possibility of mauling his old friend with his bare hands.

"Well, that's up to you really. You can either join us, which I'd advise, or we can wipe your memory of the last day or two and drop you off at home. You won't remember any of this and things will go back to how they were for you."

"Who exactly is 'us' and how long have we been here?"

Matt took another step into the room, momentarily regarding Haley before looking back at James. "We're the Consciousness Liberation Front, which I'm sure you've heard of by now. And as for how long you've been with us, probably around three or four hours."

"So you're a terrorist now. Wonderful. Welcome back from the dead."

"A terrorist?" Matt scoffed. "Hardly. We're freedom fighters. I know, I know. One man's terrorist is another man's freedom fighter, but the public really has been misinformed about what it is we actually do."

"So you don't blow up Induction centers full of civilians in broad daylight?"

"No, we don't," replied Matt with a hint of indignation. "We ransack distribution centers and attack facilities at night. We also occasionally try to put a bullet between Dr. Nightrick's eyes, as you're probably well aware of now. Our goal has always been to end the procedure, not rack up a massive body count. Those high-casualty attacks are either Crusaders or false flag operations by Nightrick. It's impossible to tell anymore really, the two always seem to be trying to outdo each other in brutality, but the point is we have nothing to do with it. Neuro Corp is just made up of opportunistic dicks that take advantage of propaganda moments like that to discredit us whenever they get the chance."

"Yeah, I bet. Guess it's all a big conspiracy to make you look bad, huh?" said James, noticing Haley begin to stir nearby. "Look, let me talk to her about it. You're not bullshitting me about letting us go?"

"Nope, like I said you're free to leave when you want, we'll just wipe your memory a bit before you go."

"Well thanks a lot, asshole, now I won't even be able to remember my final days with her before Induction," said James, feeling a new wave of anger coming on at that realization.

"Well that's up to you, buddy. Whether or not either of you gets bound is up to you two now. If you join us, you can help us battle against the oppression that you're staring down the barrel of. Together maybe we can overthrow Neuro Corp and liberate our generation from the horse crap parade that Nightrick has started. Think about it at least." And with that, Matt turned and walked away, leaving the door open as he went.

"Great…" sighed James, looking down the dark and empty hall. "Just fucking great."

CHAPTER TWO

D r. Johnathan Nightrick sat peering out the window of the lavish office that he had built adjacent to his laboratory. The chemist watched with great interest as a squirrel battled one of its companions for a precious acorn. At the sound of a distinct chirp, he briefly shifted his attention from the contest to the luminous green AI that had risen up out of its nearby terminal.

"Dr. Nightrick, your appointment with Command is in five minutes."

He nodded, turning back towards the window. The larger rodent finally overpowered its smaller counterpart, stealing its treasured bounty. "You see that, Turing? Nature demands that its champions be strong."

"As you say."

"Tell General Bismuth to start without me, I'll be there shortly."

"Yes, Doctor," said the AI, regressing into the terminal that it had risen from.

Dr. Nightrick stood up and brushed the wrinkle out of his lab coat before making his way from his office out into the large lobby of the tower that marked the core of the sprawling complex. A crescent-shaped desk in the middle of the expansive room housed two receptionists, flanked by two richly decorated waiting areas on either side. Across the large white wall behind the two receptionists, the upside down triangle with two lines jutting from the right side that symbolized the corporation was projected in thick, black lines. Above the symbol, in gilded letters, were the words NEURO CORPORATION. He took a minute to acknowledge the huge display before pushing his way through the heavy glass door that guarded the main entrance, trying his best to avoid getting bogged down in any pointless conversations as he walked across the grounds of Neuro Corporation's main campus. Despite the swelling bustle of employees rushing all over the city-sized complex, the doctor was able to scan his way into the command bunker, which had only a small mound protruding above the surface, undisturbed. After taking an elevator countless stories underground, he finally emerged outside of the war room. On either side of the door, two honor guards stood at attention, their polished black armor glimmering slightly in the bright, synthetic light.

"Good afternoon, everyone," Nightrick said as he walked into the packed assembly. At the far end of the chamber, numerous displays were projecting all manner of facts, figures, and maps out to the occupants of the thin room. A long, metallic table, housing around thirty commanders, admirals, high ranking Neuro Corporation officials, and a few politicians who had come in from the capital, stretched down towards the far end of the room.

"Ah, Dr. Nightrick, good timing," replied the highly ornamented General Joseph Bismuth, who was standing behind a lectern at the forefront of the room. "Please, take a seat."

The general was a plump man, but his mass was more muscle than fat. He had a rather large, white mustache draped across his upper lip that gave him an almost fatherly look, despite the fire that still burned in his eyes.

Nightrick sat down at the head of the table near the door, and looked around at the gathering. Despite a sea of confident faces, an air of tension hung heavy over the room.

"First off, I'd like to say how relieved I am that you survived the attempt on your life in Dunton," said Bismuth, pausing as a round of polite applause filled the chamber. "Now, as we were discussing, the so called 'CLF' is beginning to grow again at an alarming rate. Based on the model of coil rifle used in the attack, we're relatively certain that it was one of their assassins who took the shot. The ballistics are a dead on match to our older models, which makes sense when you take into account the composition of that particular group. Originally consisting of mostly defectors from among our own ranks, the CLF nearly fell apart after their disastrous assault on Northgate. For two years they withered in obscurity, only becoming a major player again over the course of the last few months. Now they're becoming as sophisticated a threat as the insurgent Crusaders, not to mention their through the roof recruitment over the past year. Add that to the Human Liberation Army, the Free Thought Brigade, and the Raynon Reborn Army, among others, and the list of factions against us grows. The CLF was formerly content with raiding offices and local clinics. Now, however, they're beginning to go after manufacturing plants and R&D facilities as well as government registrar offices. We're now dealing with multiple fronts and multiple enemies who are all beginning to pose serious threats. We need to contain this situation before it spills into a full on civil war."

"I think it's a little late for that," said Nightrick, gesturing at the territory control grid projected out behind the general. The red lands indicating territory lost to the insurgents covered almost as much of the map (primarily the south) as the blue lands indicating regime-controlled regions. "How are they managing to successfully attack these facilities? All of our factories are heavily guarded. I can't seem to understand why you're having so much trouble squashing these homegrown insurgencies. At the rate you people are losing land, there won't be anything left to defend by the end of the year. And let's not bother calling it a civil war, that's not the right term for what's going on. It's a proxy war between the East and the West, and our people are the unlucky hosts who get to bleed as a result of it. This conflict wouldn't have even lasted a year had it not been for foreign intervention. If the rebels are in fact becoming more sophisticated, as you've claimed, it's because every nation with an ax to grind or an ideology to shove down the world's throat has decided to make their stand here. Now please, explain to me this newly observed sophistication and the reasons why no one at this table is competent enough to deal with it."

"You have a lot of fucking nerve, you know that?" said the white-suited admiral near the front of the room, turning to address the doctor. "Isn't it bad enough that we allow a child to wield so much power? Do we have to listen to him berate us too? You're thirty and you've been running the show for some eleven years now. What a lovely job you've done so far. What's your official title even? President? Emperor? King of Coren? This entire war council is a joke. Why don't you head over to one of the elementary schools nearby and see if you can find us a viable prime minister while we're on the topic, Bismuth. You want to know why there's a war going on, Dr. Nightrick?"

"Admiral Mizuno, enough," said General Bismuth, trying to regain control of the room.

"No, it's not enough. I'm tired of listening to this imbecile make decisions like he knows a god damn thing about war. You're a great chemist, Dr. Nightrick, but you're a shitty, shitty statesman. Just because Parliament gave you emergency powers during the Uprising doesn't mean you're fit to rule Coren. I feel like I must be insane, like I'm the only person who notices this. You weren't elected to do a damn thing by anyone, and I'm tired of spineless bastards like Senator Huxen over there slithering around Dovaruss like your personal whipping boy. You ended the Raynon Uprising, I'll give you that, but it's high time you stepped aside and let humanity rebuild itself."

A strained silence overtook the room for a long moment. Dr. Nightrick cleared his throat. "Is that so?"

"You bet your ass it is."

"Is anyone else of this opinion?" asked the doctor, looking around the table. "No? Let me explain something to you, Admiral, that you might not have caught wind of while you were out at sea all that time. The only reason you, or anyone else at this table, is here is because of me. Because of what I've done. You look at me and all you see is a chemist. Sure, I wiped out mental illness, cured diseases your feeble mind couldn't even begin to comprehend let alone address, but I also ended the Uprising, and I lifted our people from the rubble of Armageddon to forge a new path. I alone created Induction to stabilize and strengthen our gene pool so that we might avoid another cataclysm. I won the war that you couldn't, and I'll win this one too. Unfortunately, this time you won't live to see the end of it. Tell me, Admiral, don't you think it's odd that none of our helicopters were on patrol over the park at the time of the assassination attempt? The shooter just flew away unhindered. Why do you think that is?"

"I have no fucking idea," replied Mizuno, starting to sweat a little bit near his collar.

"And, based on the shot they took, they seemed to be under the impression we were still using grade four glass. Their rifle would have put a round right through that. Luckily, we were using grade five. It's almost as if they thought we'd gone back to the old variant. And where could they have gotten that intel?"

"What's your point, Nightrick?"

The doctor smiled. "My point is that you were the only person I told about the grade four glass. And as for the helicopters, your friend, Colonel Sulman, was in charge of that particular deployment, no? The shooter owes her a great deal. If we had known about her ahead of time, we'd of gotten all of you. Don't worry about that though, she's already on her way to the Charon Detention Facility. You honestly didn't think we'd find out about your new friends in the CLF? You don't give Central Intelligence enough credit, Admiral Mizuno." He gestured at the soldiers near the door. "Take him."

Without a moment's hesitation, the two black-clad guards approached the admiral and dragged him out of his chair. The thin man tried to wrest himself free, but he was no match for the raw strength of the doctor's honor guard.

"Find out what he knows and then put him down quickly," said Nightrick. "Consider that your severance package."

The admiral continued squirming as he was forcefully dragged out of the council chamber. "Fuck you, Nightrick! You're all sheep. He'll be the death of all of you!" he screamed as the heavy doors slammed shut behind him.

The doctor waited a moment for the sound of the raving to die down. "I want every single person in attendance at this meeting to understand something. The foremost quality I look for in my commanders is loyalty. I value it above even competence, obviously. If you serve loyally, you will be rewarded. If you choose treason, then the same fate as Admiral Mizuno's awaits you. Now, please continue, General Bismuth, and forgive the interruption."

"Err...of course," replied the general, taking a second to tap open a new map on the center screen behind him. "Like I said, the CLF is becoming more sophisticated as time goes on. Before, they used brutish tactics to vandalize equipment. Numbers and the element of surprise were their foremost tools in overrunning our positions. Now they're using weapons and technology that would require engineers and scientists to upkeep and operate. For instance, let's review the recent attack on the Valker Plant."

Nightrick grimaced.

"The Valker Plant was formerly one of the three primary production facilities of the chemicals and machinery needed to perform Induction. It was a complex of the utmost importance," said General Bismuth, pulling up the incident report on the overhead screen behind him. "In a particularly heinous attack, the CLF managed to ransack the plant, looting and destroying as they went, as well as killing scores of high value personnel. We set to work rebuilding the facility almost immediately after it fell, but reconstructing a complex of that size will take years, even with all of the technology at our disposal. Of even greater concern than what they destroyed, is what they didn't. They took a great deal of equipment with them. Prior to this incident, only the Crusaders were actively massing our machinery. We're speculating that they're both attempting to discover a way to undo the treatment. They'd have no use for those machines outside of that purpose."

"They won't be able to undo it," the doctor replied. "We've searched for ways of undoing it ourselves. As far as we can tell, any attempt at reversing the process has a very high fatality rate. The human mind isn't made to withstand that much stress. Induction is a one way street. The best they could hope to do is adjust the binding to a different partner, which is already common practice if a member of a couple dies young, and even that does serious damage to the brain in most cases. They're wasting their time."

"Well wasting their time or not, it still demonstrates that they have professionals working with them now, and we should be taking that seriously. Our country has invested too much money in this program to watch it fall apart. We need to neutralize these hostile agents, and we need to do it soon."

"I'm already working on a solution to the problem. If we lose another facility like the Valker Plant, it'll knock Induction offline for years. Every couple of months there's another play for one of our installations. All it's going to take is one more to break the camel's back. I'm going south as soon as we're finished here, and I'll be sending out orders from there. I want all of you to have the units under your command on standby. Hold your ground, but halt the offensives in the south. With the West stepping up its support for the rebels in the area, we'll take undue casualties if we try to advance any further right now. We're going to bring the rebels to us, and make sure that the foreign powers have no one left to support. I've already told Dr. Truman to prepare the Atria Plant for my arrival."

Bismuth nodded. "Is there any other business for the council?"

The doctor shook his head. "No, you're all dismissed."

"Then if I might, I'd like a word with you in private," said the general. "Everyone, give us the room please." Bismuth waited until the last senator pushed through the door leading out of the conference room to speak again. "Using yourself as bait is nothing short of madness. You could've been killed."

Nightrick crossed his arms. "The only way we find out how many people are actually involved in a plot is to let them carry it out. If we had detained Mizuno outright, we wouldn't have found out about Sulman or any of the other co-conspirators. I don't like it any more than you do, General, but in my experience, when someone is trying to kill you, your best course of action is to kill them first. In this case, we've rounded up fifteen would-be usurpers. I'd say that's worth a small risk."

"That's fine," he replied with a frown. "The problem is, you didn't get the person or persons who actually tried to kill you. It's reckless. Use a body double next time."

"No," said the doctor, shaking his head. "The people need to see that their leader isn't afraid of the savages running wild across this country. Terrorism only works when people cower. What the insurgents don't realize is that their newfound courage will be their downfall. We're going to use their bravery to break them."

<hr />

Haley looked around the small room that she'd been given. Dirty, white paint was sloughing off the wall so fast that the grey tile floor was covered in the flakes, giving it an almost textured look.

"I'm like ninety percent sure this was a janitor's closet before we arrived," said James, who was standing behind her and taking in the sad sight for the first time too. "I bet it's not too late to turn back. This is one memory I wouldn't mind losing."

Haley smiled. "Don't be a prima donna. It's got character."

"Character? And what character is that? An indigent?" he said, walking into the room. He sat down on the twin-sized mattress that was hoisted up off the ground by a rickety, wooden bedframe pushed against the far corner. "I really don't think we should be here."

"James, we talked about this already," she said, sitting down next to him on the bare bed. "We're not going to get another chance like this. If we go back now, we'll both be Inducted and that'll be it."

"But what about Dr. Karich? What if they punish him in our place? We're being selfish."

"We're surviving. I think he'd understand that. I doubt Neuro Corp would be willing to lose someone as valuable as him over grandstanding anyway. Dr. Nightrick is a lot of things, but I think pragmatic is towards the top of the list. Besides, they have a lot of history together. Dr. Karich will be fine."

James frowned. "And what about us? We're not soldiers, we're chemists. All it's going to take is one firefight and we'll both be dead. If you were to die because of this, I don't know what I would do, Haley. I can't stand the thought of losing you like that."

She smiled, crawling behind him to rub his shoulders. "Don't worry about that, babe. I have a feeling that you would definitely be the one to die first anyway."

"Oh, well good," he laughed, pushing her aside. "Guess I have nothing to worry about then."

"Naw," she replied, pulling him down towards her. "Not a care in the world."

CHAPTER THREE

M att frowned as yet another volley soared over the paper target hanging at the far end of the lonely range. The stone wall at the very back of the expanse gave a small clang as the projectile met its end against it. The three rebels stood there in silence for a moment, bathed in the dim, artificial light projecting down from the ceiling.

"You have to aim, bud."

"What the hell does it look like I'm doing?" said James, starting to go red in the face from frustration. He raised the coil gun up again and pulled the trigger, sending another slew of metal well over the intended mark.

Haley did her best to suppress the smile that she felt taking root on her face. "You're breathing too hard. Try to relax."

"Oh, is that the problem?" James snapped. "Well I'm glad I have you two here to tell me to relax. That really takes me to my calm place. Why don't you try a few?"

She shrugged and reached over for the rifle. Bringing the sight up to eye level, the young rebel paused a moment to check her mark and then sent a slug racing straight through the head of the paper man that James had been trying so fruitlessly to kill.

"God dammit," he mumbled as she effortlessly sent a second and third round through the target.

Matt laughed, patting him on the back. "In fairness, bud, most people shoot like you their first time. She's a natural."

James nodded, trying his best to avoid clenching his teeth any harder than he already was. "Look, I'm starving. Can we go grab a bite to eat please? I've seen enough of you two showboating for one day."

Matt grinned. "Yeah, I could eat. Let's call it for now."

The small group made their way from the range to the scant, concrete pit that doubled as a mess hall. The faint scent of burned oatmeal permeated the thick air of the large chamber that sat tucked away near the center of the modest compound.

"Oh, wonderful," said James, eyeing the mush laid out on the tray before him. "Grey goo again. I was really craving some more of this gunk, so needless to say this is a big relief."

Matt laughed. "It's a lot more than some of the other groups have, you know. I hear the Crusaders keep their people so hungry that they eat rats when they're lucky enough to catch one."

"At least a rat tastes like something," said James, scooping a spoonful of the paste into his mouth.

A tall woman with flowing brown hair approached the table and took a seat next to Matt.

"Hey," she said, tucking her legs under the bench.

"Hey," said Matt. "I believe you two have met my good friend Megan Mailer."

The woman flashed a small smile and aimed her fingers at James and Haley like a gun, pretending to fire at them. James felt his jaw clench even tighter.

"Nice to meet you," he managed. "Try not to shoot either of us this time if you would."

"No problem," she replied. "As long as Matt here doesn't give me a good reason to again. So how are you two enjoying Fort Condat so far?"

"It's fine I guess, if you don't mind living in squalor," said Haley. "Something you took from Nightrick, I assume? The whole place looks like it was an actual military facility before it fell."

"It still is an actual military facility," said Megan with a small laugh. "The only difference is which military is using it now. Just be glad we're in one of the above ground installations. The subterranean bases are the real nightmare. Talk about claustrophobia.

We're lucky to have enough ground-to-air missiles here to deter air raids from the regime, so we don't have to hide in the dirt like a lot of the others."

Haley nodded.

"So," continued Megan, turning towards James. "How exactly do you and Matt know each other?"

"We grew up together," he replied, pausing for a moment to take a sip of his water. "We were raised in the same apartment building, not too far from Kingswood Park actually. Matt, you're what, two years older than me?"

"Yup."

James smiled. "This piece of work just up and disappears on his eighteenth birthday without so much as a see you later. For two years, I was relatively sure that he had died and no one bothered telling me."

"Well I would've written," said Matt, grinning back. "But I didn't want you to get carted off to the Toxic Truth."

"Mighty kind of you. So Megan," said James, pushing another lump of grey paste onto his spoon. "What's your story? Are you married?"

"Excuse me?" she replied with a small smile.

"Sorry, I just noticed the wedding bands around your neck," he said, pointing at the two golden rings dangling off of the cool steel chain around her throat. "I take it they're yours?"

"Oh," she replied as the smile faded from her face. "They're not mine. They belonged to my brother once."

James lowered his head a touch. "Ah."

"When I was nine, my older brother, Frank, was forced to undergo Induction. He was one of the first wave, the guinea pigs in a sense, to be subjected to the therapy. I remember the first time I looked into his glazed eyes after the procedure, the hazel locked beneath a layer of frosted glass. It's hard to see someone you love trapped inside their own head. Two years later, the woman he had been bound to died suddenly of a stroke, which in the early days wasn't entirely uncommon among the newly Inducted. Despite my brother's animalistic devotion to his deceased wife, he was forced by law to undergo a second round of therapy because of his young age. After that, he made it another year before he collapsed too, joining his ex-wife. A 'short-out' was what the doctors told us killed my brother, but it wasn't the stroke that cost him his life, it was a deranged doctor and the idea that Frank was just a piece of meat that could be bred like a domesticated dog."

James nodded. "Nightrick will get his soon enough."

"That he will, but it's not Nightrick I'm talking about. Frank died because a man named Dr. Hernan Cortez poisoned him during the procedure.

But that's another story for another time, I think. Enough doom and gloom for one meal."

—⊷+⊶—

The blaring sirens brought James reeling back to consciousness faster than his mind could process. The young man sat there in his bed, dazed for a moment, before being nudged back to reality by Haley.

"Something's going on," she yelled over the screeching. "Let's go take a look."

"Now is as good a time to die as any other," he screamed back.

The couple made their way down the bland white hall of the barracks, surprised by the fact that no one else seemed to be alarmed by the siren. In fact, it almost seemed as if no one else even noticed it. After making their way down yet another corridor towards the heart of the complex, they found an old man sitting in the common room and watching a show as if nothing was happening.

"Hey!" screamed James. "What the hell is going on?"

The old man looked up at the young couple for a moment with a rather blank stare. "Strike team musta jus' got back."

"Why the siren?" asked Haley.

"Done with the prisoners mos' likely," he said, turning his focus back to the show he was watching.

She frowned. "What do you mean?"

"Whatta ya think I mean?"

She moved to push the point, but as she did, she was interrupted by the sound of Matt's voice, calling them over to one of the large steel doors that adorned the throughway. They walked for a long while, until they were outside of the complex and well away from the blaring sound. The trio snaked along the well-lit outer wall of the building, towards the facility's outdoor range. Off in the distance, they could see the large, steel lampposts hoisted high in the air, illuminating the swarming activity nearby. Other than that, the night sky was completely black, with the light of the moon and the stars absorbed by the thick mat of clouds hanging overhead.

"Probably should have warned you guys about that, my bad," said Matt, his usual lighthearted tone absent. "Omega Team got back to base a while ago and they brought two Neuro Corp captives."

"OK," said James, pushing forward against the gusting wind.

"We've gotten all that we can out of them," said Matt, his breath showing in the cool air. "They're to be put to death for crimes against humanity."

The group walked along in silence once more until arriving at the range. They walked through the chain link fence as the two captives were marched out in their green fatigues, each sleeve adorned with the upside down triangle with two lines jutting from the right side that symbolized the regime. One man looked to be in his forties and the other looked to be around the same age as James. The assembled crowd stood back behind the wooden barrier that isolated the range itself, looking on at the gruesome spectacle. As the charges were being read, the young captive began to weep bitterly, while the old man just stood there with a blank face. Once the judge had finished the sentencing, he asked if either would volunteer to face the firing squad first.

The old man raised his hand. Before being led off to the wall, he touched his young comrade's shoulder, giving him a small, sad smile. "I'll go first, my boy, to show you that it's not as bad as it seems."

The CLF soldiers walked the man in front of a thick concrete wall at the end of the range. On the other end of the expanse, the masked executioner walked up alongside the firing squad. "If you have any last words, say them now."

"Just this. Killing an old man makes you weak, but killing a child makes you evil. The boy is only eighteen. How can you hope to govern if you can't even understand that cruelty is weakness and mercy is strength? Justify it however you want, you're all cowards. Enjoy my blood, because you'll have none of my tears." And with that, he held his middle finger up in one last act of futile defiance.

James watched in horror as the man convulsed when the marksmen's bullets found their mark. The prisoner lay there motionless for a moment before being carried off by two masked guards. Only the blood smeared across the wall was left to remind anyone that he had made his final stand there just moments before.

When it was his turn, the boy was not so brave. He pleaded as the guards dragged him up to the wall. Standing there shaking, he gave his final words in a more pathetic fashion. "Please! I needed the money to help feed my brothers and sisters. We had nothing to eat!"

The marksmen raised their coil rifles and fired, hitting the boy all across his torso and face. He fell over, but his chest continued to rise and fall. He moaned, squirming on the ground in agony, while blood gushed out of every open wound on his torn body. His cheek had been ripped away to expose shattered teeth, which could be seen moving as he opened what was left of his mouth to instinctively draw more air into his collapsed lungs. His eyes rolled around the onlookers, searching for a kind face as the marksmen hesitated to fire again. The boy's glazed eyes met James's own unadulterated stare, locking for a moment while the executioner barked an order. The marksmen raised their rifles back up to finish their brutal task. With the sound of another volley, James watched the life drain out of the glazed teal eyes.

He stood there with his mouth open a touch, staring at the motionless body. Haley gently wound her arm around his waist, pulling him a little bit closer.

Matt put his hand on his old friend's shoulder before turning to walk away. "Welcome to the war, buddy."

CHAPTER FOUR

M egan Mailer walked around the armory in the CLF's forward command center looking for the EMP card that she needed. Her long brown hair fell into her face as she leaned over to search the bottom shelves of the seemingly millionth rack in the room. She brushed it aside and continued digging through the endless piles of junk. When she finally found the gadget that she'd been looking for wedged behind a container of rusty parts, she snatched it up and jogged out of the storage bay.

In the room adjacent to her, Matt struggled to slip a vest about two sizes too small over his wide frame. "Who do they make these damn things for, infants? This is ridiculous," he said, noticing her nearby.

She smiled. "Actually, I think they make them for people who go running occasionally."

"Hardy har har. Maybe you enjoy the feeling of your flesh wrapping around your skeleton, but I like some meat on my bones."

"Some meat? Matt, you got the whole deli there," she said, as he finally managed to pull the vest on correctly. Before he could fire his next barrage, James walked in. Sensing his friend's unease with the prospect of his first raid, Matt took him around to gear up, hoping it would take his mind off of everything.

"You're going to be OK, buddy," he said, leading James towards the ammo depot.

"It's not me I'm worried about, it's Haley. I don't like the idea of running her into a warzone. We've gotten very little combat training from you people, Matt. We've only been here for a few weeks; it's kind of crazy to bring us, don't you think? Haley and I have spent more time here in the lab than on the gun range."

"Well first off, Haley will be just fine, you're the one who can't shoot for shit, and second, it doesn't matter. It's not about your combat abilities anyway, James, it's about proving your loyalty. We're bringing you two lovebirds along to help dispose of the chemicals. We'll do any fighting if it's necessary. Last time we hit a distribution center there were only a few guys on duty and they surrendered without a fight."

James frowned. "Did you execute them too?"

Matt sighed, setting down the ammo pack that he had been examining. "Did you think going to war would be a fun little vacation? It's hard to hear it and even harder to say it, buddy, but in situations like this, the only way you make it home every night is by being the cruelest bastard on the field at that given time. People are going to die; your only concern should be whether or not it's you."

"Let me ask you something, Matt. Let's say we somehow kill Nightrick and overthrow his regime. What then? There are at least ten different factions vying for control over the same country, does the war just go on without him? Do we just fight forever until there's nothing left to govern?"

"Well, we'd form a unity government if we could ever take the capital. Each faction would share power as we rebuilt the country. Where are you going with this, James? What's your point?"

"My point is that while the CLF might be willing to share some power, maybe, I highly doubt that the Crusaders would. And come to think of it, there's no way that the Raynon Reborn would join your unity government either."

A small frown took root on Matt's face, but as quickly as it had come on, it passed. "Look, I know that last night was hard for you guys. You're new to all of this and it takes time to adjust. After seeing something like that you just sit there all night, mind racing, wondering what the point of any of this is. Next time you ask yourself that question, look over at Haley. That should be all the answer you need."

James nodded. "Maybe you're right. So you really don't think there will be any fighting tonight?"

Matt smiled. "We'll all be fine. These places aren't that well guarded, trust me."

Dazed, James sat up on his hands and knees. While his vision was badly blurred, he could still make out shapes well enough. In the back of his mind he heard his friend's voice rattling around, *"these places aren't that well guarded, trust me...trust me....trust..."* The second flashbang thrown into the room exploded to the right of him, knocking him over. He smiled through the blinding numbness, lost in his head, as his limp body was dragged behind an overturned desk.

"WAKE UP!" Matt screamed slapping him. "WAKE UP, GOD DAMMIT!"

James heard him like he was two miles underwater. Summoning all of his willpower, he succeeded in pulling his vision back into focus. He looked around the chemical storage bay that the group had managed to fight its way into. Large totes full of yellow and white liquids were stacked all over the place, with an endless sea of barrels surrounding them. No windows adorned the walls, and only one large doorway served to connect the bay to the rest of the facility. Overhead, he saw Haley staring down at him with a horrified look on her face. Matt, meanwhile, continued to lay suppressing fire over the desk.

"Well I might have miscalculated their numbers a bit," he offered loudly over the blaring sound of gunfire.

Megan grunted. "No kidding."

She tapped the warehouse's floor plans back open on the datacuff that wound around her wrist. The translucent bracer glowed a soft yellow as she slid her finger across the display. After another careful scan of the room failed to turn up any new exits, she tapped the plans shut again.

"Well, we're trapped," she said, sounding thoroughly pissed. "Nicely done, Matt, another brilliant plan! Maybe next week we can jump out of a goddamn airplane without parachutes?"

"Oh shut up, this isn't my fault," he said, fumbling with another clip. "I'm not clairvoyant; reconnaissance is your specialty I thought."

"I've been monitoring their communications for weeks. There's been absolutely zero indication that they were beefing up security."

Another flashbang rolled next to the desk. Matt slapped it away and fired another salvo over the splinter tarp that had formerly been their cover.

"Well…we're going to die," he said with just a tinge of bitter sarcasm. "I've got about half a clip left and there're at least thirty of them out there salivating to get in here."

Megan frowned. "Well nice aim, you ape, have you even hit anyone?"

"Hey, I have an idea," said James, crawling behind one of the black barrels that they had come to destroy. Keeping himself as shielded as he could, he retrieved a small vial from inside his jacket pocket. Resting within the confines of the glass was a translucent liquid that looked quite similar to water, with only the slight difference in its shimmer serving to differentiate it. He made eye contact with Haley, who gave him a reassuring nod. The young man carefully opened the barrel and poured a bit of the vial's contents in, sealing it as rapidly as he could. With Haley's assistance, he pushed the cylinder onto its side and rolled it out towards the doorway, quickly ducking behind an adjacent container as the first one slowly approached the entry.

"Shoot the barrel," he yelled from behind the second.

Matt leaned out and fired a burst into it, filling the doorway with gas. The emergency filtration fans activated in the ceiling, rapidly inhaling the fumes.

A second barrel rolled forward and Matt fired again, sending another humungous organic plume into the air. It dissipated as quickly as it had appeared, but as the cloud vanished, it gave way to a mass of bodies, some still writhing on the ground and gasping for air.

Megan stuck her head up over the desk, looking towards the doorway. "Well, it's a goddamn miracle he hit it."

"Oh shut the hell up, Megan, these masks are practically impossible to see out of. I'd like to see how good your aim is when you're under heavy fire like that."

"Matt, if I went into a coma on top of my gun I'd fire it more accurately than you."

Matt, doing his best to ignore her, made his way over to the doorway to inspect the pile of corpses that they had amassed. The struggle for air had ended by then at least, leaving a scattered load of colorless bodies strewn across the floor. The chalky white skin was so unnatural that he found himself wondering, for just a second, whether those figures before him had ever actually been real human beings. He let his eyes trace the lines of blood running down from the bulging eyes, making the men look as though they had been crying in their final moments. "Holy shit… what was that?"

"Something I've been working on," replied James, trying hard to avoid looking at the evidence of how well his compound had worked.

"It's a *hypervolatilizer*," said Haley, turning away from the twisted bodies in disgust. "It causes organic liquids to enter the gaseous state at an unprecedented rate."

"Yeah, I can see that," Matt responded with an almost morbid tone of respect. "See, James, it's a good thing we brought you two along. Megan here must be disappointed that another one of her attempts to get me killed has gone south."

"Matt, I don't need to attempt to get you killed, you're constantly trying to do it yourself."

"Blah, blah, blah, blah," he replied, giving her the finger. "Let's get this done with and get the hell out of here before more of these bastards show up."

CHAPTER FIVE

The gruff-looking commander circled the thin metal table of the interrogation room, taking a deep puff from the thick cigar he held in between his forefinger and this thumb. His green fatigues and black combat boots, along with the thin stubble projecting out of his otherwise bald head, gave him a rather prickly look. The deep lines etched into his face shifted as he frowned.

"I'm going to ask you one last time what that liquid was and where you got it, then I'm going have to do some things that we're both going to find unpleasant."

"I already told you, it's a hypervolatilizer, and I synthesized it myself. Now what have you done with Haley?" replied James, looking around the cramped cellar. Mildew stains marked the craggy walls, and the only source of light streaming into the room was from a grate that rested up near the ceiling.

"We need to know where you got that compound from, because right now, you're looking an awful lot like a security risk to this organization. If someone sent you, all you have to do is tell me who it is and this will all be over."

"I synthesized the compound myself and nobody sent me, you assholes abducted me."

"Look, kid, I don't want to do this but you're really not giving me a lot of options here," said Commander Fluron, setting a ball-peen hammer down on the metal table in front of him.

James scowled. "I'll prove it, but there's not a whole hell of a lot I can do chained up here. If you want to see whether or not I'm telling the truth, you have to give me access to a lab. Sitting here and threatening me with a hammer isn't going to get you shit."

The commander regarded his prisoner for a moment. "You want access to a lab? Fine. But if you can't produce that compound like you say you can, I won't be using the hammer on you. I'll be using it on your little girlfriend."

"I swear to you that if you touch one hair on her head, I'll take that hammer and gouge your eyes out with it."

"Big talk for an unarmed kid," said the commander, taking another puff from his cigar as he moved towards the door. He called out into the hallway, gesturing towards the table. Two masked rebels entered the room, scooped up James, and carried him out into the corridor. As they carted him along towards one of the two labs located at Fort Condat, he scanned every passerby for a friendly face. Most of the other rebels just turned away and avoided eye contact as his procession marched by.

"Cowards," he said to no one in particular.

When the group finally reached the lab, they released him.

"Make it," said Fluron. "And you two, go grab the girl. I want to make sure that our recruit here is adequately motivated."

James looked around the small, earthen lab. One workbench sat in the middle of the room, and a few shelves lined the walls, holding various chemicals with little organization.

"You couldn't take me to the nice lab?" he said, picking up one of the jars of powder and examining the label.

"The nice lab is for people we trust. You get the pit."

James set the jar back down. "I guess I'll make do. And for the love of God, put that cigar out before you kill us all. This is a lab, not a fucking bowling alley."

The commander gave him a nasty look as he tossed his cigar onto the floor and crushed it with his black boot. "There you go, safety lad. Now get to work."

James grabbed the nearest volumetric flask, rinsing it with acetone in the nearby solvent sink. He pulled the various jars and containers that he needed off of the shelves, carefully measuring each reagent with the old scale before adding it into the flask. Slowly, he mixed his compound back into existence, lost in his head while he worked. When at last he looked up again, he saw Haley standing in the doorway, flanked by the two brutes that had dragged him into the lab.

"You're missing something I need," said James. "I can't create the hypervolatilizer without the Karrion catalyst."

"Well I hope for her sake that that isn't true," responded the commander.

"James," said Haley, widening her eyes a touch. "Stop toying with them and just add the final reagent. You know as well as I do that the Corrak catalyst can be substituted for the Karrion."

The young chemist hesitated for a moment. "But..."

"It works, doesn't it?"

He nodded. "Fine."

He pulled the small vial of catalyst off of the top shelf and added a precise amount into the solution.

After shaking the glassware for a moment, he sucked a few drops of the product up into a syringe and then corked the flask. He leaned over and grabbed the last jar that he'd set on the bench, pouring a clear liquid into one of the nearby beakers.

"Watch," said the young man, pushing two drops back out of the syringe and into the isopropanol that he'd poured for the display. As the drops hit the surface, he quickly covered and shook the beaker, then released it to the open air. Only vapor rose up before the assembled group, leaving no trace of any solvent behind.

"Like I told you," said James. "Now can we please go?"

The commander smiled, walking up to the workbench and picking up the corked flask. "Yes, I'm sorry I ever doubted you. You're both free to leave just as soon as you write down the instructions to make this little wonder."

Nightrick sat in his lab at the Atria Plant musing over the data laid out in front of him. He watched the footage of the raid again and then reviewed the readout from the filters. On the screen, the 3D structure of the hypervolatilizer spun freely in open space. The doctor touched the display and rotated the structure to get a better look at the opposite side. "Turing, pull up the results from the last ten formulation trials. I think maybe where we're running into our problem is in solvent selection."

"Right away, Doctor," responded the entity.

"Perhaps we need to try something a bit more polar. Use Acetonitrile, but keep everything else constant. Let me know the second that the products are finished."

"As you wish."

The AI dissolved back into its hub, causing its green glow to fade. Nightrick heard the machinery in his lab grind back to life as the entity began running the next battery of experiments. He peered through the glass into one of the adjoining labs at Dr. Truman and his team, who were also hard at work trying to solve the enigma. On the hub in the lab, the Atria's resident AI, Edison, was speaking to some of the other chemists about extending the temperature range of their trials by another 2°C. There was something thoroughly off-putting about the blood-red glow that emanated from the AI's visage. The doctor was half tempted to shut Edison down and have him reformatted by someone more sane and trustworthy, but the pragmatist in him wouldn't allow for it. Doing so would cost a fortune and greatly reduce the Atria's output during the repairs.

The beady, milky brown eyes of Dr. Truman scanned over one of the flasks that he was working with before handing it to his research assistant. Truman had about twenty years on his employer and was the very definition of physically average, except for his tendency to sweat almost incessantly. Cold, hot, it didn't matter; the man was always soaking through his shirts and dabbing away beads of perspiration while he worked. Every lab coat he owned was stained in his own signature pattern from all of the bodily fluid that leaked out of him daily. His body looked like soft dough, but he stood upright with a pride that made his employer feel even more disgust when looking in on him.

Nightrick made eye contact with him, signaling for the sweaty man to come into his office. Truman walked in with the same pompous strut that made his boss want to chop off his legs every time he saw the arrogant display that his employee made of something as simple as walking.

"I can't figure it out!" he stared. "We've been at it for weeks and I feel like we're not much closer than we were when we started. Whoever made that volatilizer is quite clever. Perhaps if we could just use Edison instead of forcing our two AIs to share the network, we'd have a greater chance of success."

"I trust Edison as much as I trust you, Truman, which is not at all. I didn't bring Turing along for the fun of it. You're lucky I even allow that monstrosity of yours to continue operating the Atria Plant."

"With all due respect, sir, if you want me to run this plant effectively, you have to trust my judgement."

"Do you know why you run this facility? Because you're the best in your field. That's it. If I had my way about it, I'd have had you executed years ago for using my procedure as some sick tool to poison people. You're a serial killer and you've done nothing to earn my mercy or my trust."

"Was a serial killer, Dr. Nightrick. If you recall, you cured me of my baser instincts before reassigning me here."

Nightrick nodded. "So I hope. You've made sure that my lab is equipped for the procedures?"

"Yes, sir, the equipment is just about ready for use. All you'll have to do is the routine neural mapping of the patient beforehand. Why, may I ask, do you need to be performing Inductions and other reprogrammings at this facility?"

"That isn't your concern, Truman," said Nightrick, frowning. "You've finished reinforcing the structure, I hope? If this plant falls, Dr. Truman, I will personally be the one to end your life."

"Of course. Not even Special Branch could overrun this location now. It's absolutely invulnerable. And, I assure you that by the time I leave the Valker Plant, it will be as unbreakable as the Atria."

"It had better be. You're dismissed," said Nightrick, waving away the soaking blob standing before him. With that, Dr. Truman marched out of the office. He made a grand show of returning to his laboratory, making sure that everyone in the room was aware of his return from handling important business with the boss by obnoxiously parading back to his station. Nightrick shook his head as he retrieved a pen sitting nearby on his desk. The doctor began scribbling down his umpteenth theory for the reaction mechanism when his phone went off. He considered silencing it for the fourth time, but a nagging sense of responsibility swayed him in the other direction. "General Bismuth, I've reviewed the footage of the raid again. I've seen that boy with the compound before, I'm sure of it. He was there that night in Dunton. Whoever he is, he's absolutely brilliant... and dangerous."

"I'm telling you right now, there's no way in hell that kid made that. They've got a new chemist somewhere and we need to get our hands on him before he does some serious damage."

"A chemical prodigy isn't unheard of."

"You aside, I have trouble believing that kid is capable of this. According to the report I got back from Central Intelligence, his name is James Mercer and he just turned eighteen. He's actually an employee... errr, former employee of Neuro Corp. The kid disappeared with his girlfriend and fellow employee,

Haley Hall, a few days before his birthday. That's her in the video with him."

Nightrick's brow furrowed a touch. "Hardly a coincidence, the CLF preys on that dividing line. What project were they working on before they disappeared?"

"Apparently they were assigned to the IMMORTAL Initiative, project 2137, working under Dr. Omar Karich on photosynthetic cells."

"Really?" said Nightrick, leaning back in his chair. "I haven't seen Omar in ages. Perhaps it's time we caught up. Does Mercer have any family that might be able to help us locate him?"

"Report says he's an orphan, adopted by Dr. Karich at age six."

"Adopted? Omar never mentioned anything to me about a son. How curious. Bring him to the Charon Detention Facility. I'll be on my way there shortly. I want to meet this James Mercer."

Megan and Matt approached James and Haley as they keyed their way out of the large lab in Fort Condat.

"Hey, guys," said Matt with a friendly nod. "What's up?"

"Oh, just unwillingly helping our slave driver mass produce the compound I designed," said James with a sigh. "What about you two? You seem...happy?"

Matt smiled. "We finally found him. We found the bastard."

"Found who?" replied James, sliding his keycard into the front pocket of his lab coat. "What are you talking about?"

"Dr. Hernan Cortez, the chemist responsible for killing my brother," said Megan. "Or as he's known now, Dr. Truman. Nine years ago that asshole was responsible for overseeing Inductions in my hometown of Claynor. If you were to do a search on him now, you wouldn't find much, except that he'd been assassinated five years ago by Crusaders. That would be fine if it weren't for the fact that he's alive and well and responsible for literally hundreds of short-outs that could have been avoided. See, Hernan liked to amp up the volume of the chemicals that he used in the procedure so that many of his patients suffered strokes following the treatment, my brother and his wife among them. While short-outs were fairly common back then, his rate was nearly fifty percent and it didn't take long for him to catch the eye of his superiors. The sadistic animal was carted off to prison, where he was supposedly killed during an attack by the Crusaders. However, two years ago a defector from Neuro Corp let us in on a little secret. Hernan didn't die that night. Instead, he simply vanished into thin air and no one had any clue where he'd gone. Until now, that is."

Haley raised her eyebrow. "Well where is he?"

Megan leaned in a little bit. "From what we've gathered, he's serving as the head scientist at the Atria Plant now. I owe Dr. Truman a visit. Only problem is we'd never be able to break into the plant and kill him there. The place is literally a fortress. It would take a full army to even begin to mount an attack. But going there won't be necessary. We have it on good authority that Truman is traveling out towards the Valker Plant in three days to help oversee the next phase of reconstruction. We're going to intercept him en route and show him that though he was gone, he was never forgotten."

"And how exactly did you find this out?" asked James, trying his best to avoid frowning.

"Nightrick isn't the only one with spies. I don't know if the intel is any good or not, but I'm not going risk letting that bastard get away again. My brother deserves justice. Now usually we'd put a strike team together for this sort of thing, but given the target, we need to keep everything hush-hush. Truman is too high priority, and if he catches wind of anything, he'll either avoid making the trip, or bring a larger force. Either way, it'll put him out of reach. I need people I can trust. We're going to be surgical about this."

"Well then..." James replied with a sinking feeling in his stomach. "Looks like it's back into the field."

CHAPTER SIX

Megan and Matt continued their grueling descent down the steep, rocky hill towards the abandoned highway below. The desert camouflage the two had donned danced lightly in the warm wind blowing down through the elevations on either side of the road. Overhead, the sun beat down in an unforgiving torrent of heat.

Matt wiped away a bead of sweat that was dripping down onto the thick, dark-lensed goggles he had positioned on his face. "If we don't get down there soon I'm going to vomit. Why the hell did James and Haley get to stay with the jeep while I had to come down here with you?"

"Well," Megan started. "Probably because James and Haley have never set up a laser relay before, but you have. Having them come down here with me would be pointless."

Matt grunted. "It's not rocket science, Megan, you just position the two nodes on either side of the highway, make sure they're perfectly aligned, and program the desired height."

"And if they're not aligned properly, the weapon won't activate and Dr. Truman will drive right through unhindered, which is why you're here and they're not. Now stop bitching, you're wasting energy."

"Pshh, whatever. I still can't believe Command is letting us try this. You must be closer with General Harkon than you let on," said Matt as he huffed his way down the last stretch of the descent. The duo paused for a moment, taking in the barren road, shadowed by the cliffs looming over it.

"It wasn't Harkon that authorized the attack, it was Commander Fluron. He probably appreciates that we're not going to get another shot at Truman while he's this exposed."

"That might be it. Or maybe he's hoping to get rid of us," laughed Matt.

Megan smiled. "Or one of us anyway. Alright, this should be good. If we can tuck these in at the bend here, they'll be practically invisible."

She tossed Matt one of the two metallic nodes out of her rucksack. Snatching it out of the air, he examined the cylinder for a moment, then crossed the single lane highway that led through the pass. A sharp spike jutted out from the bottom of the instrument, and a circular indent with a thin metal tube rested near the top. He stuck the cylinder into the ground and tapped his datacuff, bringing the node online.

"OK," he said. "Ready for alignment?"

"Roger," she replied, swiping her finger across the display on her own datacuff. "Relays are synchronizing. Move yours left by five degrees."

Matt tapped the command into his cuff then swiveled the metallic cylinder until his readout flashed. "Should be good. Input the height and give it a shot."

Megan's finger flourished across the display, bringing the relay online.

The two cylinders shot up on either side of the highway and fired off a high powered laser line that would bisect any vehicles coming through the pass when activated. After ten seconds, the beam faded and the spikes on the nodes began to retract, returning the cylinders to their original height, just protruding above the sandy surface.

Megan nodded. "OK, I think we're ready. Now all we need is Dr. Truman."

James and Haley sat huddled together near the lightless generator that was emitting a cozy heat into the frigid night air near the jeep that they had arrived in. Overhead, the moon and the stars shone brightly down through the cloudless sky. James looked around at the open expanse stretching far away from the plateau. Only sand and darkness met his gaze. He smiled as he felt Haley shift a little closer, resting her head against his chest.

"Happy birthday," he said, putting his arm around her. "I wish we were somewhere nicer to celebrate. Eighteen is a big one."

"Where would you have taken me?" she asked, looking up at him with a smile.

"Oh, I'd probably have given you a pack of smokes and a bottle of bourbon, and we'd have gotten drunk on your porch," he said with a big grin.

"Stop," she laughed, hitting his chest lightly. "It's too romantic."

"I know, I know. I'm a real sweetheart. But seriously, I was thinking maybe we'd have had lunch in Kingswood Park, underneath the giant oak tree where we met. Then I probably would've have taken you across town to that gallery they were building when we left. I'm sure it's open by now. You'd of loved the paintings, I bet, and I would've pretended to, because I love you. After that, I'm guessing we would've gone back to your place, and lay out in the backyard like we used to, staring up at the stars all night and dreaming about visiting them one day. I guess we get to do one of those things at least."

"I'm just happy that we're here together. We made the right choice."

"Here," he said, leaning over and reaching into his rucksack. "I got you something. It's not much, but I hope you like it." He pulled a small book out and handed it to her. "It's a brief history of Coren. I would've gotten you something nicer, but…"

"I love it," she said, flipping through the pages for a moment before setting it down. "It's perfect. I can't wait to read it when we get back to base."

He gave a small nod, but the smile had faded.

She studied his face for a moment. "What's wrong, babe?"

"It's just… I don't know how I feel about all this, Haley. Is this really who we are now? We just drive around killing random people?"

"The man's a murderer," she responded, looking into his eyes. "The world will be better off without him."

"I hate to break this to you, but we're not exactly innocent anymore either. Who are we to decide whether this man lives or dies now? I don't even know who I am anymore, Haley, or who I'm becoming. I don't think this war is ever going to end by us slaughtering each other. There are no spoils of war if everything burns along the path to victory. This is nothing like we planned it."

"We always talked about the future like we had one already. But we were never guaranteed a future. We have to earn it. If we don't fight the war now, while we can, then there won't be a future for us."

James sighed. "You know as well as I do that we can't go back to Fort Condat after this. Our time in the CLF is done."

"I know. Once they realize that the formula we gave them for the hypervolatilizer is unstable, they'll probably kill both of us."

James nodded. "Unstable is an understatement. With the Corrak catalyst, that formulation probably has a half-life of around two minutes. I've been telling them for weeks not to use any of the compound that they've been synthesizing because it has to age before it gains full stability, but I can tell they don't believe me. They've produced tons and tons of the stuff, Haley. When they realize that they've been mass producing nothing more than a useless solvent, we'll be lucky if all they do is kill us. Once Dr. Truman is dead, we have to get away. I think it's best if we don't tell Megan and Matt."

"I agree."

"So where will we go? I've been thinking maybe we could go back to Dunton, for a little while at least. It'd be nice to get home, even if it is just for a short visit."

"And be detained? I don't think so, James. We need to find our way into the Free Thought Brigade, that's probably our best option right now. At least there we should be relatively safe until we can figure out a better plan. They've been operating on the outskirts of the country for years. They're hardly on anyone's radar anymore."

James moved to argue, but before he could get a word out, Haley pulled him in, pressing her soft lips up against his. When they finally separated, she lay down on the blanket next to him.

"Guess that's that," he mumbled, leaning back. He put his arm around her and closed his eyes, falling into a trance-like sleep.

The young chemist found himself looking out across an empty vacuum, floating freely in the ether. There, in the distance, he could make out a fire dancing wildly through the abyss. He willed himself towards the light, and his body responded by swimming into the flames. As he drew nearer, he could tell that the source of the blazing fire was Haley, her hair burning brilliantly without being consumed in the inferno. Her back was turned to him as he floated up next to her. He reached out for her shoulder, fearing the inevitable approach of her melting visage, as the chemicals began to warp his reality. But to his horror, as he turned her around, his eyes met her once turquoise stare, now dulled by the glaze that coated it. He spun around to face the mirror, only to find that it was he who was melting away this time. His features slowly oozed off of his face as he looked on in disgust. He tried stopping the flow with his hands, but he couldn't halt the current no matter what he did. The flesh just kept slowly slopping down until it reached a deep, viscous sag, and then it began to rescind back onto his head. When the last of the tannish goo had solidified, he looked out on himself again. This time he recognized his features, but they were blurry and distorted, as though he'd never be seen correctly again.

He woke up in a frenzied panic, shooting onto his feet as fast as his body could manage it. His heart raced as he looked out over the mesa, into the darkness. To his relief, he saw the light emanating from his friends' equipment as they trudged back into sight of the camp.

"Whoa, bud, relax, it's just us," said Matt, breathing heavy as he walked over and set his pack down near the truck.

"Sorry," mumbled James. "Must've been dreaming."

Matt smiled. "Lucky bastard, getting to sleep. I've spent the day on a lovely hike with Megan here, who needs a surprising amount of breaks for someone who likes to bust my balls about fitness."

Megan set her pack down next to Matt's. "Matt, I offered you those breaks because I didn't think I'd be able to carry your ass up that incline if you finally gave out halfway up."

He rolled his eyes. "Oh I'm sure."

"Look, why don't you two get some sleep," said James. "I'll stay up for a while."

Matt patted him on the back. "Much appreciated, brother."

"Yeah, thanks," said Megan, walking over to her sleeping bag.

And so James sat down, alone in the camp for what felt like an eternity, watching the sun rise in a cascade of pink and red. He barely noticed it as he reflected on the return of his nightmares. Haley woke up a few hours later and joined him for a modest breakfast. They ate their bland cereal in silence, with an unspoken understanding floating between them. By midday, he had returned to normal, laughing and teasing like he always did, but as twilight approached, he couldn't keep his eyes open any longer. He dozed off as Matt and Megan began their third game of chess for the evening. Just as he started to float through the vacuum that he so loathed, he felt himself being shaken. He woke up with a start, looking out across the plain at headlights approaching.

"This is bad," said Matt, who had woken him up. "No one should be out here, especially this goddamn late. It's nearly four a.m. The convoy must have sent out scouts."

Megan had already taken up a firing position behind one of the heavy truck doors, with Haley on the opposite side cradling her own coil rifle.

"Shit," James said as he wiped the sleep out of his eyes and reached for his own weapon.

"Put your damn guns down, are you guys crazy?" hissed Matt at the group. "If they alert Truman's convey, we're never going to get another chance at him. Just let me do the talking here. I'm great under pressure."

Megan rolled her eyes, but lowered her weapon all the same. "Fine, I'll jam their transmission signal and prep an all clear ping, just in case your no doubt brilliant brand of diplomacy goes tits up."

She leaned into the truck and started fidgeting with her datacuff while Haley and James quickly covered their rifles with blankets nearby. As the charcoal black, armored truck pulled up, Matt approached the vehicle with a friendly smile. Two equally black-clad soldiers hopped out, wearing the signature fatigues of Special Branch. The men were relatively unarmored, not bothering with the usual full suits of plate or helmets. They had handguns holstered to their sides, but didn't concern themselves with anything bigger.

"Gentlemen!" Matt started. "How can we..." One of the men grabbed him by the arm and swung him around, slamming him hard into the hood of their armored truck. Pinned down and with the wind knocked out of him, Matt did his best to continue.

"I believe there must be some misunderstanding," he huffed out with what little air he could spare. "How can we help you on this lovely evening?"

"You're all being detained," said the soldier who was pinning him to the truck.

"For what exactly?"

"For breaking curfew and suspicious activity. You have no business being out here in the middle of the night."

"We're camping. Come on, guy, cut us some sla…"

Matt felt the solider pull him off of the hood and knee him square in the chest, knocking the newly returned air back out of him. He gave a pathetic wheeze as he fell over onto the ground. The soldier moved to kick him, but Megan was quick on the draw. She tapped the all clear ping on her data-cuff, then leaned back into the truck and pulled her concealed rifle out of the driver's seat. Leveling the weapon, she opened fire on the soldiers. Both men drew their pistols and returned fire, quickly moving to cover behind their own vehicle, leaving Matt squirming along on the ground.

"Oh shit," said James, scrambling to get his rifle back out from hiding. He grabbed his weapon and tossed the second rifle over to Haley, who had taken up position behind the open door of their jeep. Megan leaned out from her own cover on the other side of the vehicle and fired off another salvo towards the armored truck. As she did, return fire rushed past her, clipping her exposed datacuff. Tiny slivers of metal and glass rained down from her otherwise guarded wrist.

"Fuck," she said, hitting the damaged cuff in a fruitless attempt to bring the display back online. "Matt, you have to input the activation sequence."

Matt crawled against the front of the armored regime truck, caught between the two parties exchanging slug after slug. Off in the distance, he could just make out a stream of lights rounding the bend in the road, approaching the ambush point. *Shit*, he thought, noticing his datacuff lying on the ground in between the two groups. *Must have come loose when I went down.*

"HOLY SHIT!" he yelled, jerking involuntarily as the headlight next to his actual head exploded from the impact of a stray shot. "Could you assholes aim? And while you're at it, WOULD SOMEONE THROW ME A GOD DAMN WEAPON PLEASE? "

Megan stopped firing long enough to toss a handgun out over the door that she was ducking behind. It landed just in arm's length of Matt, who greedily scooped it up. He went prone and squeezed a shot off into the first black boot that caught his eye. The rebel marksman was rewarded with a yelp, as the wounded soldier hobbled back in pain.

"Matt, it's now or never. Activate the fucking relay!" shouted Megan.

He looked back out over the highway and saw that they were about to miss their one shot at Truman. Pushing back onto his feet, he lunged out of cover towards the datacuff, slapping the device towards Megan as he came down near it.

"Do it now! Do it now!" he yelled to her. She snatched the still functioning cuff out of the air and punched the code in as fast as she could, bringing the system online. Matt had just enough time to hear the weapon relay fire up and rend metal before the blinding pain of the bullet passing through his body caused him to black out.

"Matt!" screamed Haley, spinning out from cover to lay down suppressing fire for her wounded friend. As she finished emptying her clip, she too was struck, taking a shot clean across her upper torso. She spun from the impact, hitting the side of the jeep that she had been ducking behind.

James watched as Haley's limp body fell into the sand next to him. Blind with rage, he darted out from cover, firing wildly and charging straight at the hostile position. Megan did her best to cover the mad rush, sending another torrent out from behind the riddled door she was shielding herself with. Halfway across the expanse that lay between him and the regime fighters, James heard his rifle go dry, but he pushed on all the same.

As the soldier who had shot Haley realized the enemy fire had let up, he leaned out from behind his truck door and squeezed off another volley at James, hitting him twice. The young rebel stumbled and dropped his empty rifle into the sand, but didn't seem to realize that he had been struck as he regained his footing and flew at the door, ramming full force into it and pinning the man in between his vehicle and the metal that he had been using for cover. James heard a satisfying scream from his assaulted foe as he rounded the door, quickly bending low to grab the fallen pistol. Without a moment's hesitation, he spun, firing a clean barrage into the other already wounded soldier, killing him instantly. The young rebel then turned his attention back to his last remaining target, bringing his foot down hard on the man's shin. A loud crunch filled the air as the bone gave way, sliding out of position. He grabbed hold of the wounded soldier by the dark cloth of his shirt and tossed him aside with a bestial strength. The man landed in a heap, rolling onto his stomach and trying to pull himself across the sand, away from the jeep. James took a moment to check the clip of his newly acquired handgun before walking slowly towards the now sobbing soldier that was desperately crawling away from him. Realizing that he'd never escape, the man rolled over to face his pursuer, as James brought the barrel of the pistol up to his head.

"Please, please!" moaned the soldier, raising his arm as if to shield himself. "I surrender."

James spat on the man who he'd seen shoot Haley, then pulled the trigger. As he heard the dull thud that emanated from the projectile parting flesh and skull, he felt something new welling up inside of him, an animalistic pleasure as his opponent's life slid out through the back of his head. The feeling passed, giving way to lightheadedness. James looked down at the dampened sand, illuminated by the light of the moon, and realized that the thick red soup staining it wasn't just the soldier's blood, but his too. He smiled for a moment, lost in his own head, before collapsing into darkness.

CHAPTER SEVEN

D r. Nightrick studied the glowing monitor in-
tently, trying to get a read on his old friend.
*He doesn't look like he's changed much since the Uprising.
His hair is as dark as ever, a bit thinner maybe, but he
still looks ready for war. I guess some people never lose it…*

The doctor crossed the hall and entered the
small detention room that his captive was being
held in. The chamber was empty, save the table, two
chairs, and camera tucked into the rightmost corner
of the cube. He flashed a warm smile. "Omar, it's
been too long."

"Or is it not long enough?" said Dr. Karich. "You
know you could have just asked me to come, I wouldn't
have denied you. The theatrics of stealing my records
and kidnapping me were totally unnecessary."

"Maybe, but your adopted son has been confirmed as an agent of the Consciousness Liberation Front. I wasn't sure where his allegiances began and yours ended," replied Nightrick, sitting down across from his captive.

"You weren't sure of my allegiance? I thought I made it pretty clear when I saved your life eleven years ago," said Dr. Karich, looking down at the plain metal cuffs binding him. "And was it really necessary to chain me to the table?"

"I've seen what you can do, Omar. It was very necessary," said Nightrick with a small smile. "But in the interest of keeping this friendly, I'll untether you." The doctor tossed his old friend the keys to the cuffs. "Do you know where we are right now?"

"I have a few guesses," he replied, working the key into the rusted slot on the left cuff. "Based on the bland décor and the archaic method of confinement, I'd guess that we're in one of your prison complexes. Based on your penchant for the dramatic, I'd guess that it's the Charon Detention Facility."

Nightrick nodded, allowing a moment for the fact to settle in.

"I remember the rebels used to call this place the Toxic Truth," said Dr. Karich without the faintest intonation of fear. "They said that if you had a tight lip, the sadists here would be more than happy to remove it for you. Apparently your people are enthusiastic about their jobs."

"They're not my people really. I gave control of this complex over to Special Branch near the end of the Uprising as I transitioned into the main campus. I never really cared for the heat here. The Brukan Desert is absolutely sterilizing. Good for keeping prisoners in, but unpleasant to say the least. I don't know how the people over in New Haven can stand living near this giant oven."

Dr. Karich finally managed to turn the rusted lock, freeing his left arm. "Well, from what I understand of things, you run Special Branch now, so in effect any installation of theirs is still an installation of yours. I never took you for someone who would tolerate the mentally unstable manning one of your facilities. I thought you were more about curing lunatics than encouraging them."

Nightrick tensed up, doing his best to hide it. "The only way to deal with an extremist is with an extreme response. Who better to interrogate and break lunatics than other lunatics? In my opinion, anyone who maintains the old adage that you can't fight fire with fire has never heard of back burning."

Dr. Karich smiled at his old friend's retort. "There's the sharp wit I remember so fondly. Glad to see that not everything has changed."

"And yet so much has. Tell me, Omar, how is it that you came to be a father? Don't take this the wrong way, but I never really thought of you as being cut out for parenthood. You were always more of a fighter than a coddler."

He laughed. "Is there a right way to take that? The Uprising turned more children into orphans than I care to think about. I promised the boy's parents a long time ago that I would watch over their son if anything ever happened to them. As for me, I never wanted to be a fighter or a coddler, but the war made soldiers out of everyone who survived it."

"So it did," nodded Nightrick. "Now, as much as I've enjoyed the pleasantries, let's get down to clearing things up so that we can get you back to work, Doctor."

"As you wish," said Dr. Karich, finally managing to free his other hand. "If you brought me here to ask me where James is, I can honestly tell you I have no idea. But, between you and me, even if I did know, I wouldn't tell you. He's my son, John. I've seen how you handle people that you consider threats."

"I'm not going to allow innocent people to die because you want to protect your child from facing justice for his crimes. James was involved in a very deadly raid a few weeks ago on one of our processing plants. Your son killed nearly thirty people with a chemical weapon. He then proceeded to destroy literally tons of valuable chemicals and make off like a thief in the night. He used a volatilizer of his own design and we have reason to believe that he's begun producing said chemical weapon for the CLF, which, as I'm sure I don't have to tell you, is a capital offense and a breach of the Darion Conventions. Now listen to me very carefully, Omar. Your son is a brilliant chemist and I respect that. The boy could have a bright future at Neuro Corp, but I can't help him if he continues to aid and abet terrorists."

"I have trouble believing that you're interested in helping him," said Dr. Karich, rubbing his wrists where the harsh metal had chaffed his skin. "Anymore, I think the only person you're interested in helping is yourself."

Nightrick shrugged. "Even if that were true, working with your son would be beneficial to me, and so naturally I would be willing to overlook his past indiscretions if I could convince him to join me. I have the power to pardon whomever I please. If I will it that James's crimes go unanswered, then that's exactly what will happen. Sometimes true justice isn't about getting even, but finding something good in the wake of something bad. The boy is young and impulsive, which is an inclination I understand all too well. When I was his age I was fighting a war of my own. I did a lot of stupid things at that point in my life and I'm lucky that I survived to see the end of the conflict. If it hadn't been for some of the people that I looked up to, I might well not have. I see a lot of myself in your son. I want to help him, but I need you to make that possible."

"Let me be as clear about this as I can possibly be, John. If you expect me to side with you over my son, you can go to hell. If that means that I have to suffer in his place, so be it."

"So be it. Perhaps tomorrow you'll be more open to reason. I'll be back at dawn," said Nightrick, standing to leave. As the doctor exited the room, he sealed the door and grabbed the first technician that he could find. "Ensure that our guest is more inclined to speak to me tomorrow. Be as gentle as he allows you to be, but under no circumstances are you to let up until he's feeling more agreeable to sharing what he knows with us. Understand?"

The technician nodded and smiled the same sadistic smile that the doctor had seen over and over again on every face that he'd encountered since arriving.

Nightrick frowned as he walked away.

"Turing," he called. He watched as the AI rose from the nearest hub, casting its brilliant green light against the reflective metal walls of the hallway. "Keep an eye on the rabid dogs running around here. I meant it when I said that I didn't want Omar excessively harmed. If any of the interrogators go overboard, I'll have their head for it."

"Yes, Doctor," replied the AI.

"I'm beginning to remember why they call this place the Toxic Truth."

⊶⊷

After days on the road, the ravaged rebels finally made it back to Fort Condat in the dead of night. Megan brought her jeep to a halt just outside the rusty double doors leading into the small medical center attached to the facility, and hopped out.

"Megan, glad to see you made it back in one piece," said Commander Fluron as he approached with the emergency response team that she had called ahead for. "Is everyone still alive?"

"For now. I was able to stabilize Matt and Haley pretty well before throwing them into the jeep. I think their wounds are superficial. James though... James is a different story. He took a full burst across his chest. It's a miracle that he's survived for this long, to be honest. I did my best to stop the bleeding before loading him, but I'm not exactly running a triage center here and I had to get us away from the ambush site as quickly as possible. After we were safely away, I started pulling over every half an hour or so to try and stem the bleeding, but no matter what I did he just kept leaking out onto the floor."

The medics opened the door of the jeep and pulled James out first. His skin was pale white, save the blood smeared all over the front half of him. His chest just barely continued to rise and fall as they laid him down across the stretcher.

"Wow," said Fluron, taking a puff of the thick cigar he had tucked between his forefinger and thumb. "I wouldn't hold my breath, he looks horrible. I'm not sure they're going have the resources here to do anything for him."

"We'll do our best," said one of the physicians that had appeared next to the gurney. "Let's get him inside and get to work. I'll send another team for the other two shortly, as long as they're stable."

Megan nodded, and the group wheeled the young chemist off into the medical center. "This is all my fault. The attack was too rushed. We didn't have enough time to plan things out like we should have. If he dies..."

"Then he dies having proven himself loyal," said the commander, exhaling another cloud of smoke. "At least we'll know that we can trust him then. Don't beat yourself up, Megan. I feel bad about your friend, but you guys took out one of the top officers in Neuro Corp. That's worth bleeding for. Hell, it's worth dying for."

Dr. Nightrick looked up from the notepad that he had been scribbling on as he heard a knock against the heavy oak door that led into his private chamber in the inner sanctum of the Charon Detention Facility.

"Come in," he said, watching the door swing open before one of the numerous attendants that served the upper echelon at the facility. The servant took a moment to straighten his grey blazer before introducing the newcomer. "Sir, the Director of Central Intelligence here to see you."

"Thank you. Leave us."

The attendant bowed, closing the doors behind the spymaster.

"Welcome to the Brukan Desert, Director Fox. I hope this trip down here was worth your time," said Nightrick, standing to shake the man's hand.

Dario Fox nodded, grasping the doctor's hand in a firm embrace. His black suit and brimmed cap were tailored with the great care of a man who valued appearance as much as substance. He wore his thirty years of service well, with a thin face that had a certain reptilian quality to it, except for the warmth that radiated from his eyes. He sat down on the other side of the doctor's lavish desk, taking in the rest of the opulent furnishings. Beautiful paintings, a four post bed, and, of course, the magnificent cherry desk, all standing in sharp contrast to the rest of the wretched prison that lay just beyond the walls of the chamber.

"Forgive the interruption, Dr. Nightrick. I know how busy you've been these last few weeks, but I wanted you to hear this directly from me. Three nights ago, around four in the morning, Dr. Truman's convoy was ambushed on the outskirts of Tanzeer."

Nightrick's jaw tightened. "A Western airstrike?"

"No, sir. It appears to be the work of one of the insurgent groups operating in the region."

"Of course, no women or children died so it couldn't have been the West. Which group is responsible and what is the condition of Dr. Truman?"

"We believe that the CLF is behind the attack. The insurgents used a laser relay to slice the vehicles as they drove around a particularly sharp bend. The weapon matches those used in similar attacks by the group over the last few months. The relay is crude, but it bypasses our vehicle's armoring in a way that conventional improvised explosive devices couldn't. As for the condition of Dr. Truman...He survived, but barely. He's in critical condition right now after being airlifted back to Dovaruss."

Nightrick rubbed his forehead. "Keep him alive if you can. I don't give a damn about Truman, but I don't want the CLF taking credit for another high profile assassination. They're getting bolder by the day. We need to capitalize on all of this naked courage that the insurgents are finally feeling or they're going to overrun us with it. I need you to do something for me, and I need it done with the highest level of discretion."

Fox leaned forward in his chair. "Anything, Doctor."

"I want you to leak to the Crusaders that Dante is to be executed at this facility within a fortnight. Once you've done that, leak to the CLF that Dr. Omar Karich is to be hanged alongside him."

Fox nodded. "As you wish."

"Once you've finished, I want you to head back to Dovaruss and keep a sharp eye on any buildup in or around New Haven. I want to know when the Crusaders are coming to pick up their prophet."

Matt rubbed his thigh again where the metal had torn through his skin. "I hope James is doing OK."

Megan sat down next to him in the mess hall, setting a white tray with a big mountain of grey gunk on it down in front of him. "Eat up."

"How's Haley doing?" said Matt, picking up the spoon. "You saw her again last night, didn't you?"

"Yeah, she's fine I guess, or as fine as she's going to be until they release James anyway. I wish I could get her to eat something, but she hasn't left the med center in days. She just sits there with that book he gave her, waiting. At least I can always count on you to eat."

Matt gave her the finger as he shoveled a spoonful of the paste into his mouth. "Glad to see your wit made it through unscathed. I heard Commander Fluron left the base yesterday with Omega Team."

"Yeah, what of it?"

"Well I noticed they took a shit ton of that hypergobbalizer, or whatever the hell they call it, with them. I told Fluron when I talked to him last that he should wait for James before using any of it in the field, but he basically told me he wasn't going to wait for a dead man to rise up and give him permission to do his job."

Megan shrugged. "I'm sure James would be happy to hear that his hard work in the lab is being put to good use."

"Yeah, well that doesn't change the fact that Fluron is a twat. I think he'd fit better with the Crusaders personally. The dude is a nut job if you ask me." Matt scooped up another spoonful of grey paste. "Anyway," he continued. "We ought to go check on James later and see how he's doing."

"Yeah," said Megan, feeling the cool metal of the two wedding bands dangling around her neck brush up against her skin. "I hope he's getting better."

Haley paced back and forth in the tiny, worn down lobby of the medical center at Fort Condat. She paused for a moment, then approached the front desk for the umpteenth time.

"How much longer until one of you people can tell me something?" she asked. "It's been six days and I haven't heard a word from any of you. I want some information."

The nurse sitting behind the counter scowled. "As I've told you a hundred times now, all I can say is that your boyfriend is alive still. Other than that, you're going to have to wait for Dr. Kayfez to finish up. Why don't you go back to your room for a little bit, get some sleep, take a shower, and have a bite to eat? You look like a zombie, dear."

"I'm tired of waiting. You go tell Dr. Kayfez that he can either come out here and speak to me or I'm going back there to speak to him. And if you try to stop me, you'll become a patient in your own med unit."

The nurse huffed, but got up and went into the back all the same. When she finally returned, a tall, weary looking man walked out into the lobby with her. His dark skin stood in sharp contrast to his white lab coat, which had been stained red and brown in the unending onslaught of patients brought to him every day.

"Ms. Hall, sorry to keep you waiting for so long," said the doctor. "James has kept us quite busy these last few days."

"How is he?"

"He's stable now. I didn't think he'd make it through the first night, to be honest, but he's a fighter. We've managed to retrieve all of the metal from his torso and stem the immediate threat to his life. There were some complications, however."

Haley frowned. "Complications? Like what? Is he going to be OK?"

"Like I said, he's fine for now. The damage to his upper chest was severe though, and we had to use nanotech to seal off his internal bleeding and stimulate tissue repair. Normally after a round of treatment like that, the bots are siphoned back out of the body via a modified dialysis machine, but at the present time we don't have anything like that here. Frankly, he's lucky we had the bots in the first place. The regime left them behind when this complex fell a few years ago. The point is, I was forced to shut down the machines while they were still inside of him, using an applied electrical field. They should be harmless now, but you'll notice a rather severe discoloration across his upper chest tracing the path of his cardiovascular system. I'm not sure what sort of effect that will have in the long run, but at least he's alive."

"I can live with a scar. When will he be able to leave?"

"Today, I suppose. He needs to take it easy for a while and give himself plenty of time to recuperate, but he should be fine to go home."

"Awesome," she said smiling. "Let's get him out of here."

⸫⸪

James ran his finger along the lightly displaced tissue on Haley's shoulder as he stared up at the ceiling of their room, if you could call it that. The chamber was small, with just enough space for a bed and a dresser. Haley was fast asleep next to him, worn out from the exhausting days behind her and content with the fact that her love was safe and home at last. He had tried resting too, but he couldn't escape the thought of those unfortunate men, gasping for air as they died in agony. The air caught in his lungs for a moment, but he pushed it back out and tried to calm himself. His chest pulsed, seizing lightly. He closed his eyes and saw the nameless, faceless soldier, begging for mercy that was never coming. Their twisted faces, one by one, continued to flood through his mind in graphic detail, stuck on repeat. He diverted his gaze to Haley, lying there so peacefully. He studied her, trying desperately to remember every gentle, subtle hill and valley to her form. She was so beautiful, so unspoiled by the decay that now surrounded them. As he sat there, entranced in her glow, he realized that some things were in fact worth killing for.

And with that, he fell into a dark, dreamless sleep. Peace at last.

His slumber broke off suddenly as he was shaken awake. Matt stood over him with a warped look on his face. As Haley stirred nearby, he started in. "Buddy, there's been news while we were away. The other officers wanted to keep it on the D.L. but I thought you deserved to know."

"What?" James replied, rubbing the exhaustion from his eyes. "What are you talking about, Matt?"

"Dr. Karich has been arrested. He's being held at a detention facility for conspiracy to commit high treason. Word is he's going to be executed in your place."

James felt his stomach lurch.

Matt frowned. "Command only knows about all this because the information was leaked to us, very purposefully we believe. It's an obvious trap."

James sat up. "So what's the plan? How are we going to free him?"

"We aren't," said Matt, diverting his gaze. "The facility was nearly impenetrable before. Adding to the fact that it's an absolutely blatant trap, Command has decided that it'd be best not to throw our army against the rocks. I'm sorry, bud. We've been losing too many people lately and an attack like that would be the end of the CLF."

James threw up over the side of his bed. Haley sat there without flinching, rubbing his back.

"You can't be serious?" he said, wiping the spittle from the corner of his mouth. "You people can assassinate a high level chemist but you can't help free my father?"

"Killing a lightly guarded, high priority target in transit is one thing, but running our entire army into a trap is another entirely. In one clean swoop they could wipe us all out."

"I have to go. They want me, not him. This was all a huge mistake, I should have just gone through with Induction and moved on with my life."

Matt shook his head. "It's no way to live. I'm sure your dad is happy you escaped. Don't let his sacrifice be in vain."

"I'm going."

"No. No you're not. If they mean to capture you, it's probably because your little compound put on quite a show a while back. Giving yourself to them is suicide. They'll find out what you know and then they'll kill you and your dad anyway."

James stood up and pushed past him, making for the door. Halfway there, Matt shoved the needle of a small syringe into his neck, squeezing the clear liquid into his friend. "You'll thank me for this eventually, bud."

"You fucking trait..." James trailed off as he slumped over onto the cold tile beneath him.

Haley lunged off the bed, landing squarely on Matt's back. The extra weight caused him to stumble, tripping over the now limp body of James. The entangled duo came crashing down, with Matt slamming tooth first into the bed frame. He spit out blood and chips of his teeth as he lurched to throw her off of him. He couldn't quite get a grip on her though as she wrapped her arm around his neck and began to choke the life out of him from behind. His vision narrowed as he flailed desperately at her, but she continued to pull tighter and tighter. As the last bit of light left his eyes, he heard gunshots ring out, and the world faded to black.

CHAPTER EIGHT

He didn't need to open his eyes to tell he was moving. James felt every bump in the road as firmly as if he was being dragged behind the vehicle that he'd been tossed into. As his mind began to race with possibilities, a familiar voice served to reground him.

"His face was messed up badly enough as it was, did you really have to shatter his teeth?" said Megan.

"I honestly didn't mean to break him like that, he tripped over James," Haley replied. "I feel bad about it, but in fairness, he shouldn't have tried to stop us from leaving."

At the sound of her voice, James sat up and opened his eyes. He looked around for a moment before realizing he was in the back seat of Megan's jeep. There was a large brown stain running from the leather upholstery of the seat down to the carpeted floor. Outside, the world was black, but for a thin sliver of light just starting to break on the horizon.

"What's going on?" he managed.

"I saved all three of you, that's what's going on," said Megan, turning the steering wheel left at another bend in the road. "I tranq'd these two loud asses and made off with the lot of you before anyone else could get to your room. Command is going to be pissed off something fierce when they realize we're gone."

"Three of us?" said James, turning around to find Matt still unconscious in the back seat, bound with rope. His face looked like an orange that had been wrung for juice. A few thin streaks of blood were leaking out of his mouth and pooling onto the carpet of Megan's jeep, adding to the mosaic of bodily fluid accumulating on the vehicle's floor.

James frowned. "Why would anyone else be trying to get to our room?"

"Well..." started Megan. "Right after Matt left the intelligence briefing to come tell you about your dad, reports started flowing in about an explosion that had taken place during one of Omega Team's raids on a distribution center just outside of Alawez."

"What the hell does that have to do with us?" asked James, leaning forward in his seat.

"The reports said that Commander Fluron tried adding that compound you've been making into some chemical container or another to neutralize the products. When he did, the entire container exploded, setting off a chain reaction that killed ten of our people. Command is of the opinion that you intentionally sabotaged the compound and they wanted to put you up against the wall for it. I knew right away that there had to be some kind of mistake, so I quietly snuck out of the meeting and came to get both of you, only to find Matt getting his ass whooped by Haley here and you blacked out on the floor already. After breaking that up, I quickly loaded all three of you into a cart, and for the second time in as many weeks, chucked your unconscious asses into my jeep and made off like a thief in the night. Haley explained the missing catalyst to me while you were out. You guys should have told me, but it doesn't matter now, I guess."

"Shit...Well, where are you taking us?" he asked, looking out the window at the passing trees rising up against the backdrop of the desolate desert that stretched behind them.

"Well, I figured we'd go get your dad. We've got nowhere else to be right now. Frankly, the CLF will probably be putting a nice fat bounty on all of our heads anyway, so the safest place for us right now might actually be the Charon Detention Facility. Besides, I owe you for helping me with my little excursion. As for Matt, I haven't quite gotten his take on things yet because he's pumped full of enough tranquilizer to sedate an elephant, but seeing as we're halfway there already, he can either join us or walk back and try to explain what exactly he was doing in your room when I got there."

"They can put him up against the wall for all I care. That rat bastard tried to stop me from leaving."

Megan laughed. "If you call what he did 'trying', then I suppose. If he had any sense at all, he wouldn't have told you about it like that, but Matt doesn't think sometimes. I'm not sure why he thought he could wake you in the middle of the night, tell you two what he did, and then restrain you from leaving with one syringe full of sedatives. It'd almost be comical if it weren't for the fact that he probably thought he had a really solid plan. He's going to be pissed about his teeth, but like I was explaining to Haley here before you woke up, he was obviously never much to look at before, so he hasn't lost too much really. Well except for a few teeth and whole lot of his dignity."

She looked back at James, who was scowling out the window at the passing road. "I know you might not believe it, but I'm sure Matt thought that what he was doing was for your own good. You're like a brother to him."

"It isn't Matt's place to interfere with my personal life. I would burn the world to ash and glass if it meant keeping my family safe. He had no right to try and stop me. With what authority did the CLF bind me? None. None at all."

She shrugged. "Maybe, but then again what gives any group authority really? Power. Whether you like it or not, the CLF now considers you to be a saboteur. On top of that, this little trip is what we would call desertion. If they ever catch us, we'll be suffering the same fate every other prisoner in this war faces at some point or another. I'm afraid that we've crossed the Rubicon. Anyway, sit back and enjoy the ride, we'll be there in about three hours."

Twilight broke as the ragged band pulled into a charging station some twenty miles outside of New Haven, cradled on the border of the Brukan Desert. As Megan hooked the jeep's power cells up to be recharged, James stepped out into the crisp night air to clear his head and escape the insufferable sounds of Matt. While Megan had had the foresight to hog-tie him, she had unfortunately neglected to gag him as well. Matt hadn't allowed his battered mouth to silence him, despite acquiring a distinctly new accent. He'd woken up about an hour ago and had been alternating between cursing them all and making sweet promises to aid them at least twice a minute.

The sky above swirled into a milky purple as the death throes of day gave way. James heard Matt screaming something about having to take a piss as Haley opened her door to join him. They stood there in silence, enjoying what they both knew was the calm before the storm. The group was poorly equipped for an operation of such magnitude and everyone there knew it, including Matt, who had spent a good ten minutes yelling about how they stood a better chance of vaporizing an ocean with a heat lamp than breaking into the Charon Detention Facility with their present equipment and number. If Megan was nervous, she wasn't showing it. In fact, she looked more like she was on vacation than preparing to go into battle. She had been assuring everyone that she had a plan to sack the facility since Matt had started in about it. After finishing recharging the vehicle, she opened the trunk to find Matt squirming all over the place trying to free himself.

"Look, if you don't untie me and let me out of this car right now, I'm going to literally piss myself," he said.

"I'll untie you if you promise to behave yourself, Matt."

"What am I going to do at this point? My face feels like it's on fire and I'm unarmed in the middle of goddamn nowhere."

She pulled a long, sharp knife out of the sheath strapped to her side and cut the rope free around his hands and legs. He came bounding out of the trunk, half running, half hobbling off into the bush to relieve himself. As he came sauntering back, he started in again. "So what's this miracle plan of yours? I guess I have to help, because I'm pretty much implicated in this bullshit now either way. Besides, you three are definitely going to die without me."

Megan grinned. "Yes, Matt, what would we do without your flawless marksmanship and award winning smile?"

"Hardy har har. Please tell me that your entire plan isn't to berate me until the war is over."

"Look, I have a friend out here who's been working on attacking the complex for ages. In light of recent developments, he's going to be assaulting the facility at the same time we're trying to. He's assured me that together we'll be able to sack the Toxic Truth."

Matt rolled his eyes. "Oh, you have *a* friend? Well then, please disregard all of my previous complaints and concerns, I'm sure this will go very well for all of us. And here I was carrying on, never realizing that your plan was based on having *a* friend. Sounds great."

"This friend of mine is a Crusader, and we share a vested interest," she replied, crossing her arms. "He's the leader of the Archangels, one of their special ops teams."

Matt's face paled out into the color of curdled milk. "I know who the fucking Archangels are, Megan. I see we haven't quite finished betraying the CLF just yet."

CHAPTER NINE

Michael Drake ceased his incessant pacing to look out across the bleak horizon of the Brukan Desert for a moment, before turning back into the living room of the apartment he shared with his brothers to address them. All three of the siblings had the hard bodies of men tempered in war, though Raphael, who was sitting on the saggy yellow couch next to his younger brother Gabriel, dwarfed both of the others. The rundown quarters they shared reeked of mildew, but it was inconspicuous in that.

Michael took a step towards the ratty couch. "I'm telling you right now, Raphael, ripping a door off of its hinges because the sound annoys you has all the subtlety of shooting a man because you don't like the color of his shirt. It's like you're going out of your way to draw attention to us."

Raphael shrugged. "It was squeaky and I was tired of it. I thought it'd be better to have one big noise than a million tiny ones."

"I can't seem to get you to understand that we're trying to remain incognito," said Michael, holding on to what little patience he had left. "I know that this is the longest period of time that we've ever just sat around, and I know that this shithole apartment is about one small step above destitution, but getting sloppy now will only guarantee that we wasted our time coming here."

"Your little plan is taking too long. We bullshit around here all day, rotting, while Dante does the same damn thing a short drive away. We could have been in and out of Charon with him before they even knew we were there and we could have done it months ago."

Michael shook his head. "You've seen the prison layout, same as me. You know good and well that there's no way in hell anyone could sneak in there and sneak back out undetected. The place is a fortress."

"Oh? They say the same shit about the Atria Plant, but we managed to capture Dr. Wan there all the same, now didn't we?" replied Raphael, leaning back on the dank couch. "And if I'm remembering correctly, didn't we blow General Frasier's head off while he was sitting in his office, clueless that we had snuck into his supposedly 'impenetrable' headquarters? You're sitting here giving me this load of shit about how we can murder the top officer in Special Branch but we can't break into some shithole prison in the middle of nowhere."

"Years ago, before the Valker Plant and the Reach fell, that kind of thing was possible. Now that Nightrick's force is consolidated, things are different than they were back then. Let's see how well any of that would go now. We're good, but we're not that good. You don't seem to understand that sometimes wars need to be fought with armies."

Raphael grunted. "And sometimes they don't. When was it exactly you lost your sack? I thought I was talking to my older brother, not my little sister."

"And I thought I was talking to a cognitive human being, not a big lumbering ape. Guess we were both wrong" replied Michael, going red. As Raphael jumped up onto his feet to attack his brother, Gabriel finally spoke, causing both men to halt in surprise.

"Michael is correct. Even when we leveled the Reach, we needed the army to back us up. The once mighty, central hub of chemical distribution that linked the Valker, Rikon, and Atria Plants fell, sure, but we didn't do it alone. Michael's plan isn't flawless, but when it comes to attacking an installation such as the Charon Detention Facility, it's as good as it's going to get."

Raphael sat back down with a sour look on his face. "We owe it to Dante to get him the hell out of there. How much longer are we going to wait?"

"I've already summoned the primary strike force," said Michael. "Dr. Reya informs me that everyone who's coming has been deployed."

Raphael frowned. "Oh really? And why now, suddenly, are you so anxious to attack?"

"We don't have a choice anymore. Word from headquarters is that Dante is going to be hanged within the next week. Besides, I promised an old friend of mine that I would help her attack the facility. With the group she's bringing, we'll never have a better opportunity than now."

Raphael's face twisted. "Don't you dare. Don't you dare tell me it's who I think it is."

"It is."

"Give me a damn break, how stupid are you? And how many of those CLF cunts is the bitch bringing with her?"

Michael frowned. "Watch it, Raphael. Don't push your luck with me. She's bringing three other people along with her."

Raphael rolled his eyes. "Four people? Wow, nicely done, Mike. Way to build bridges. You've always been blind and stupid when it comes to her. All your damn thinking takes place in the head between your legs when she's around."

Michael moved to punch his brother, but once again held off as Gabriel spoke.

"Raphael is correct. She makes you do stupid things, and bringing them along is surely going to be one of them. It's folly to pour gunpowder into a fire and not expect it to blow up in everyone's faces."

⊷┤┝⊶

The barren sand continued to race by as Matt looked out his window again with the same mien of unease that had been etched across his face for most of the trip. He watched as an old burned out factory rushed by, cloaked in the shadows of twilight. "So how do you know this guy again?"

"We met a long time ago during the assault on Northgate, the northernmost corridor into the capital," said Megan, turning the steering wheel left towards the faint outline of the city looming in the distance. "This was a little bit before your time, Matt. Had we been able to break the line there, we might have been able to march on Parliament and end the war."

"I'm aware of Northgate, Megan, thank you very much. What, do you think I crawled out from under a rock to join the CLF? That battle was the whole reason I joined up in the first place. After I saw that you guys had given Neuro Corp a black eye, I started believing that just maybe, somehow, Nightrick could be brought low again."

"They weren't the only ones who got a black eye that day. Bismuth's army was pushing our force back with relative ease thanks to their air superiority, so my fire team was deployed to knock out the air defenses in the western quadrant. If the CLF could have gotten its handful of fighters into the sky, we might have stood a real chance at breaking the blockade."

Matt nodded. "That goddamn air force is one of the only reasons that Nightrick has held on this long."

"Yeah, and it'll probably remain one until the war has ended. Anyway, things went well for our squad at first. We made it into the control room with little resistance and disabled the anti-air cannons. For a minute it looked like we might actually crush Bismuth. As each fire team reported in that they'd succeeded, Command launched our entire fleet against the position for what we hoped would be the defining battle of the war, and it may well have been, considering we lost our entire air force in the ensuing chaos. I knew we were screwed the second I realized that the turrets were still firing despite our having 'knocked them out'. It was too late though, the trap was sprung. As our fighters flew in, they met a wall of anti-air that shredded almost the entire fleet of the CLF. But it wasn't just *our* planes that were taking a beating. The Crusaders seized on the opportunity and deployed as well, not realizing that we hadn't actually accomplished anything. They flew into the same slaughter that we did, but they were lucky enough to be following us in, so they were able to pull back a few of their fighters and begin shelling the positions from a distance."

"I'm not aware of any Crusader air force," said Matt, interrupting once again. "There's no way that they still have any craft left."

"No, they lost their entire fleet in the ensuing battle, but at least their pilots got to fight back. Our guys just got massacred. At that time they didn't have the manpower or knowledge base to maintain an air force anyway. It was more of a distraction for the ground teams than anything else. They were lucky if they could even keep their planes in the sky, to be honest. But like I was saying, Dante sent the Archangels in to do what we had tried to do, and destroy the cannons guarding the skies around the area. Naturally, they succeeded. By that time, my squad was trapped between Special Branch and the advancing Crusaders, and we were risking being buried alive by staying in the crumbling control center. We lost about half our group on the way to the roof, but we pushed on until we couldn't advance any further. Our position was overrun by Special Branch and we were all about to die when the Archangels fell from the sky and saved us. As their main strike force engaged Bismuth, we were extracted with Michael and his brothers."

"*Wow*, fell from the sky huh? OK, first off, I'll remind you that those 'Archangels' are the same people who have worked tirelessly to kill us and our friends in their crazy town parade," said Matt with a hint of venom. "You know, friends of ours like Jon Rain, who they beheaded in cold blood after the Battle of Draynok. Where was all of this mercy and kindness then? And secondly, why *would* they save you? Unless they didn't know you were CLF."

"They knew, though Gabriel and Raphael weren't pleased about any of it. Michael and I spent what time we could together after that, short though it was. He's the reason that I could never bring myself to hate the Crusaders despite all of the horrible things they've done. I tried my best to turn him, but at the end of the day, he truly believed that they were on the right side of things. I haven't seen him in years, but we still keep in touch every now and then. Before I came back to the CLF, I asked him why he had saved us. He said it was because he'd never seen anyone as beautiful as me."

"Oh my God, I'm going to be sick," replied Matt, rolling his eyes. "Well now at least we know that the Archangels are blind."

Megan punched Matt in the arm as hard as she could manage while driving.

"Oww, goddammit," he said, rubbing his bicep. "I'm just kidding, but seriously, this isn't going to end well for us. These people are legitimately crazy, why do you think we don't work with them more often?"

And for that, she had no response.

Dr. Nightrick walked over to the large window in his private chamber and looked down on the small courtyard below, tucked safely away within the inner sanctum of the Charon Detention Facility. One stone bench, a small pink-leafed tree and an old weathered statue of some hero or another from the Uprising were all that adorned the enclosed space.

"He's dead?" he repeated in shock.

"Slipped away last night," came Bismuth's voice through the receiver. "Considering how injured he was it's amazing we were able to keep him alive for this long, to be honest."

"I don't know if I should mourn him or throw a parade. I mean on one hand I've lost a gifted chemist, but on the other, the rabid animal who bastardized my creation got exactly what he deserved. Whoever did it, they probably did me a favor in the long run. Now I can finally wash my hands of that disgusting sweat sack."

"I thought you might be pleased. No one else here at the Atria Plant knows yet, but I'm sure once they find out that Dr. Truman is dead, it's going to be a madhouse for a little while."

Nightrick rubbed his forehead. "Well, I suppose you should inform Dr. Mason that he's been promoted. I'd do it myself but I'm a bit busy here. Central Intelligence has informed me that they've detected a large host forming around the outskirts of New Haven. The group is doing very little to hide itself and I'm certain that the timing is no coincidence. I think the Crusaders are finally preparing to pay me a visit. I just hope that Mercer is with them. From what Director Fox has told me, the CLF has placed a rather large bounty on the boy's head for treason. Maybe he's finally seen the beast for what it is."

"Are you sure you don't want me to reinforce that position? If the Crusaders hit hard enough, not only will we lose Dante but we might lose the entire facility."

"No, if we lose Charon then so be it. I can't risk giving them a bloody nose here or they might hold back when I need them to go all out. There's a large enough force here for me to hold the inner sanctum. I *want* them to have Dante back. Only he would be bold enough to try and assault the Atria and stupid enough to use his entire army doing it. The only way this ever ends is if I let that lunatic go home. Hope is the armor that shields the flame of revolution when its fire is burning low. Once I break the Crusaders and take their hope away, they'll melt into oblivion where they belong. It's Mercer I'm concerned with now. I think Dr. Karich will see things my way once the boy arrives. If he can convince his son to join us, then we'll be one large step closer to finishing off the wounded CLF and restoring order."

Michael stood on the stoop attached to the five-story apartment complex, bathed in the dim yellow light cast out by the nearby lamppost. He watched as the bullet-riddled black jeep pulled up against the curb directly in front of the building.

"Welcome to paradise," he said, approaching the vehicle as Megan hopped out of the driver seat.

"Nice place," she said, looking down the deserted street. "Did you ask your realtor for the bubonic plague special?"

Michael smiled. "Only the finest for the Archangels."

"No doubt. I'd like you to meet my friends Matt Donner, James Mercer, and Haley Hall, formerly of the CLF."

The Crusader nodded at the trio as they climbed down from the vehicle. "Pleasure."

"Likewise," mumbled Matt. "Maybe we can finish the pleasantries inside? I'm concerned I'm going to catch cholera if I stand out here any longer."

"Of course, follow me," said Michael, gesturing towards the door. "We're on the third floor. Don't be alarmed by the smell, that's just the charming scent of New Haven."

After a brief climb, the group walked into the small apartment that Michael shared with his brothers. An old foldout table had been set up near the saggy yellow couch, along with four folding chairs for the newcomers. Old wallpaper was peeling up all over the place, revealing white drywall wherever it had been ripped off. A small kitchenette sat off to the side of the living room, and a short hall branched off into three equally small rooms, two bedrooms and a bathroom.

"Wow," said Matt, staring down the hall. "How long have you guys been trapped here?"

"We got to New Haven about six months ago," said Michael. "And by the way, this is my brother Gabriel."

The youngest Archangel looked up from the book he was reading on the yellow couch to nod at the newcomers.

"I thought there were three of you," said James, moving to sit down at the foldout table with Haley and Megan.

"Raphael took off about an hour ago. I wouldn't count on him being back tonight. He's not thrilled with the extra company."

Matt nodded, taking a seat next to James. "I hear that. Must be hard sharing your home with a bunch of infidels."

Michael shrugged. "We've done worse."

Matt smirked. "Oh, I'm sure of it. Tell me, Mike, if you don't mind me asking, how did you three end up in the Crusaders? You don't look much older than me, but I've heard stories about how you were some of the very first people to take up arms against Dr. Nightrick. How is that? Did the Crusaders let children fight in their army from the very beginning or is that a recent development?"

Megan's face went beet red, but Michael smiled at the snide question.

"Well, Matt, you're about half right. My brothers and I were there at the rallies all those years ago, back before the protests against Induction had spilled into full on violence. I'm twenty-five now, but at the time I was sixteen, Raphael was fifteen, and Gabriel was fourteen. You should have seen it, thousands of people in the streets, chanting, screaming, marching, all those voices swirling together into one to demand that Dr. Nightrick step down and that the government cease the implementation of Induction. There was an electricity in the air, a sort of endless hope. But it gave way as soon as the first shots rang out. Then panic and fear were all that remained. Some people ran, some people hid, hell, some people even started throwing rocks back at the aggressors, but all I know for sure is that after Special Branch opened fire on the crowds, our fate was sealed. My brothers and I watched the riot police drag our bloodied father off to some nameless, faceless detention center, never to be seen again. So what choice were we given? We joined up with the Crusaders for one simple reason, Matt. Blood for blood. Now if you'll excuse me, I think I'm going to go get some rest. I would suggest that all of you do the same thing. We have a busy day ahead of us tomorrow."

CHAPTER TEN

Dawn broke early that morning in New Haven, scattering the light of its star through the clouds like shattered glass. Haley sat staring out the window of the black jeep that she'd been assigned to, looking out across the wasteland masquerading as a city. The melancholy buildings had seen the rise and fall of the once mighty metropolis. She couldn't help but wonder if they might one day recall their rise and fall as well, if the attack went anything like Matt continued to insist it would.

Behind her, in the backseat of the jeep, Megan and Matt were fast asleep. Thanks largely to the field medics that the Crusaders had brought with them, Matt's head, resting on Megan's shoulder as he dozed, was beginning to look less like a battered orange and more like a human being. They'd even managed to give him a temporary dental mold to replace his badly damaged teeth. He almost looked normal again, with a faint smirk beginning to return to its natural state of existence across his face.

Turning back around, she looked out across the staging area that the Crusaders had chosen on the outskirts of the city's historic manufacturing district. Hundreds of men and women had flocked to the area over the course of the night. The pilgrims came from far and wide, eager to pay homage to their god through blood and steel. They loaded up their bandoliers with grenades, strung belts of ammunition through the chain guns hanging off the back ends of their assault vehicles, prayed, and waited devoutly for their opportunity to overrun the infidels and rescue their prophet from certain death. As she scanned the sea of warriors, clad in a million shades of yellow and black, she noticed James approaching from the makeshift command center the gathering force had established in a derelict old factory that stood starkly against the backdrop of the looming desert.

"Well, it looks like we're almost ready to get underway," James said, waking the slumbering duo in the backseat.

"What exactly is the plan here?" asked Haley. "We're going to just charge head first at the facility?

They'll know we're coming the second we set foot outside of the city."

"They probably already know we're here. There's been literally zero effort to mask the incoming traffic. For better or for worse, Michael seems to think it won't matter whether they realize we're coming. This far south the regime can't deploy its air force without risking anti air fire from across the border, so all we have to worry about is what's right in front of us. I'm not a huge fan of the plan, but you're not actually too far off. The majority of their force is going to assault the facility head on, and a small group of us are going to use the diversion to break into the complex from a side access point. Michael assures me that he's familiar enough with the prison's layout to get us in without too much hassle."

"How many people are joining us in the breaching party?" Megan asked, stretching as she righted herself in the backseat.

"It's us, the Archangels, and one of their physicians," said James.

"This is suicide," Matt mumbled, wiping the sleep from his eyes as he too righted himself. "How the hell long do you think they're going to be able to distract the guards with a frontal assault? They'll all be dead within an hour, and then we'll be joining them."

"That's only half the problem anyway," said Megan. "With Nightrick there, the place is bound to be absolutely swarming with Special Branch. Have they even taken that into consideration?"

James nodded. "They believe that their force is capable of holding long enough for us to get our people out. We don't really have any other options. There's no ideal time to attack Charon. At least doing it now, the Crusaders will bear the brunt of the assault."

Megan nodded in agreement, though her ill feelings lingered. The group looked towards the old factory as the buzzing crowd grew deathly still.

"We leave in ten!" yelled Michael to the assembled army as he stepped through the wide, badly rusted double doors of the command center. "CLF deserters, follow close behind me, we're going in hot."

"That's one way of putting it," murmured Matt, opening up his bag to make sure that he hadn't forgotten anything. As he finished rifling through his equipment one last time, he noticed Raphael come walking through the same wide doors that his brother had just used. The brute of a man had avoided the rogue CLF agents since their arrival, choosing instead to spend the night out in the city. The Archangel noticed Matt staring at him, and made a beeline directly towards their group.

"Megan," he said, walking right up to the jeep. "How shitty to see you again."

"Raphael, you haven't changed one bit," she replied. "Still the sweet talker through and through."

"I'm so glad that my brother was able to secure such a crack team from the CLF," said Raphael, looking over the group. "I'm not sure how we would have succeeded here without a dough boy, two scrawny kids, and the siren who managed to lure Michael into the rocks by his dick."

"Listen, asshole," started Matt. "You say one more goddamn word to her and I'm going to cave your golem-looking head in."

Raphael laughed. "Oh yeah? Why don't you waddle over here and say that to my face."

"Boys, boys," said a stranger, walking in between the two. "Let's try and avoid killing each other before the raid even begins."

Raphael looked at the young woman for a moment before looking back at Matt. "I'm sure I'll be seeing you again real soon here, partner."

"Count on it," said Matt, staring right into the giant's eyes.

As the Archangel walked away from the lot, the newcomer approached their jeep, studying the group with a queer look on her face. She scanned the vehicle's occupants one by one with her dark eyes. A thin sheen of perspiration glistened on her olive colored skin as the cool air of dawn gave way to the warm, dry air that wafted in from the desert.

"Our friends from the CLF, I presume," she said, extending her hand to James. "My name is Dr. Mira Reya. A pleasure to meet you."

"Why how polite for a Crusader, I'm shocked," said Matt, earning him a nasty look from Megan.

A small smile traced the Crusader's lips. "I think you'll find that many of us aren't as bad as you might imagine, Mr. Donner."

"You know my name," he responded with a hint of surprise.

"We all do. You don't give the Archangels enough credit if you don't think that they'd brief us on the extra companions we have tagging along for this little excursion. You're supposedly an elite marksman."

Matt instantly shot an I-told-you-so glance at Megan.

"And why exactly have you been selected to join the extraction team, Doctor?" asked Megan, ignoring the stupid, satisfied look that Matt was continuing to flash her.

"Aside from the fact that I'm a talented combat medic who adds a valuable skillset to the group? There's no clear intel on what condition Dante is in. He's been locked up for a long time and given where he's being held, he's likely experienced a good deal of physical trauma. If he needs medical attention, he'll have access to it."

"I'm sure his faith will sustain him," said James.

"Everyone believes in something, Mr. Mercer, even you. I would suggest that you all stay close during the coming battle. Not everyone in our organization is as cordial to our enemies as I am." And with that, she walked back to the jeep she was sharing with Michael and his brothers.

Noticing the force beginning to mobilize, Matt took his place behind the front wheel of the vehicle that they had been given, and rolled down the window.

"James, get up there," he said, nodding his head towards the chain gun positioned on the back of the jeep. "It's party time."

"Is that really a good idea?" Megan said to him in a hushed voice. "Haley is a better shot, put her up there instead."

"And have James in here with a marksman weapon? Megan, a blind paraplegic could find their mark with that turret. I'd rather give Haley the rifle."

Megan smiled. "You know that from personal experience?"

Matt sighed. "What a wit. Just get in the damn vehicle before I come to my senses and leave you here."

As the duo continued bickering, James climbed up into the turret platform that encompassed the back end of the jeep. He swiveled the rotary base, swinging the gun around toward the front. The young rebel looked over at Raphael, who had also taken the gunner's spot on his respective vehicle, and couldn't help but acknowledge how fierce the man appeared. His hulking frame almost dwarfed the large gun that he was positioned behind. He'd be a fearsome sight to any hostile unlucky enough to get in his way. As Megan climbed into the front passenger seat and Haley took up position to his left, James activated the weapon's coils, bringing the current generator online. The turret clicked to life as their jeep went tearing out of New Haven and into the barren waste.

⸎

The sweltering, dry heat of the Brukan Desert was brutal as the early morning wore on. James fiddled with the strap on the big, dark, circle-lensed goggles he was wearing. He couldn't quite get the eyewear to sit correctly on the bridge of his nose. For as annoying as they were, he had to admit that they did a good job of maintaining visibility.

"What are we waiting for?" Matt asked while also playing with his goggles, trying to find that sweet spot. "How long does it take your people to start an at..." He winced as a massive explosion went off about a mile away at the front gate.

"What the he…" He flinched again as a second blast rang out across the open desert. Off in the distance, large black plumes of smoke snaked up from the besieged entrance to the sprawling facility. Emanating from the former gate, the circular double walls surrounding the prison seemed impossibly thick. Housed within them sat a handful of buildings that looked more like a guarded village than a prison complex. Matt stood gaping as he watched the tiny black dots on the outside of the now defunct gate run headlong towards the towering pillars of smoke.

"Car bombs," said Megan. "How archaic."

"Perhaps, and yet they still work quite well. It sounds like the primary sally port is open," responded Gabriel, as Raphael chuckled at the shocked look on their CLF counterparts' faces.

"I can't say I'm surprised that the CLF doesn't have the balls to do what has to be done," said Raphael. "There's a reason you people always shit the bed when it comes to winning battles."

"Sorry if we don't fight like you savages," Matt responded as the sound of gunfire began to ring out in the distance. "You people are barbarians that rely on cheap tricks and shock value to win a fight as opposed to actual skill."

Gabriel raised his eyebrow. "Barbarians? Call us whatever you want, we get the job done. There's no such thing as a fair fight, Mr. Donner. Killing is killing. I can't seem to understand why it should matter which method is used. Now enough chit-chat, let's get on with this."

Matt snorted. "Well frankly, I'm a little scared of getting back into the cars with you guys now. Who knows when you'll decide to ram one into a guard post and blow it up?"

"Get in the vehicle now or I'll spare you the concern and shoot you here," replied Raphael.

"Well, when you put it like that…," said Matt as he climbed back into the jeep.

The group drove up to the towering wall that housed their destination. Michael stepped out of his vehicle and began rummaging through his rucksack, pulling a thick tube out of the clutter.

"We're going to breach in a more subtle way," he said, holding the container out towards Raphael.

Matt smirked. "Of course. You three are renowned for your subtlety."

Raphael took the tube, carefully unscrewed the top, and began squeezing the contents of the container out onto the wall. The clear, jelly-looking paste began to erode away the concrete.

"I've never seen that stuff before," said Haley, stepping forward to get a better look. "What is it?"

"It's weaponized nano-paste," replied Gabriel. "Useful for all sorts of things."

Matt crossed his arms. "Well, where the hell did you guys get it?"

"We stole the design from one of Dr. Nightrick's research centers in Tarin," said Gabriel. "Believe it or not, Mr. Donner, we do have scientists and engineers among our ranks capable of production."

As the holes in the surface grew larger and larger, a purple gel began to leak out from the uncovered inner layer of the wall. Wherever the two substances collided, the purple gel enveloped the paste, hardening.

Michael tapped his fist against one of the solid purple rocks that were now filling the damaged portions of the wall. "What the hell?"

"A neutralizing agent," said Gabriel.

"No shit," said Matt, shaking his head. "Guess you can't be surprised that they know how to counter their own weapons."

Michael sighed. "They didn't mention that gunk in the schematics anywhere so it must be new. I guess they do learn after all."

"Why don't you just drive another jeep full of your own people into it?" said Matt. "That seems to work well enough for you guys."

Michael gave him an annoyed look out of the corner of his eye. "I don't think so. It looks like we're going in the front door."

Matt paled a touch. "The front door? You must be out of your goddamn mind. That'll take us directly through the battleground."

Raphael smiled. "That's right, little man. Try to keep up."

Matt frowned, climbing back into the driver seat of his jeep while the others took their places around him. "Well who wants to live forever anyway? Let's get this funeral started then," he said, ripping the jeep around toward the rising smoke.

The Crusaders came screeching up behind them, with Raphael firing a few rounds into the air in celebration of the coming bloodshed. James tightened his sweaty grip on the trigger of his chain gun, ready to open up on the first target that came into view. His heart was pounding hard in anticipation when he finally saw his first collection of enemy combatants come running around a bend in the wall to recapture a fallen emplacement. The black-armored regime soldiers were nearly on top of the small concrete guard post by the time the young rebel brought his index finger in on the trigger. The chain gun rattled off a steady stream of metal, dropping two of them instantly and causing the remaining two to pathetically crawl on until they met their end at the barrels of the very Crusaders they had been trying to flank.

James swung the turret around hard and fired another salvo into a retreating group as the damaged gate came into view around the curve of the wall. Tall pillars of black smoke danced wildly in the desert wind as the group approached the now opened inner courtyard. The young man could hear Raphael firing almost nonstop, howling like a wild animal all the while. As he turned the turret back towards the front of the jeep, he watched two Special Branch light armored vehicles come tearing out across the sundered terrain right at them.

Matt swerved to avoid crashing head first into the oncoming traffic, nearly trading paint with the hostile vehicles as he did. The enemy gunmen opened fire on their jeep as they passed by, tearing a series of holes into the thin armor that coated the transport. Matt cursed loudly as he weaved the group through the debris field that was left in the wake of the explosions. He brought one of the tires over a particularly large piece of stone and nearly sent the jeep airborne.

"Not a single word," he said through gritted teeth, jerking the steering wheel hard right to avoid another fallen chunk of the gate.

The armored cars had circled back around on Matt as he swung the vehicle from left to right in an attempt to make it a more difficult target. Michael pulled up beside one of the enemy cars, causing the gunner to try and swivel over on the new target, but to no avail. Raphael was too fast for the man, and he quickly shredded the exposed combatant, nearly slicing him in half with the steady stream of fire. The massive man then brought the barrel down on the vehicle's cockpit, slaughtering the driver and causing the car to go careening into the same debris field that Matt had just avoided.

The bloodthirsty Archangel howled with satisfaction as the car slammed full speed into the wreckage, flipping over as it did. Michael once again pulled in hard behind the second car, but had to fall back away as he was greeted with a salvo that sent shells hurtling right through the windshield at him. He let up so that he could swing back down on the armored car from a different angle. James pulled his own turret around to fire on the vehicle, but as he did, the attentive Special Branch gunner let go another barrage. The jettisoned metal tore through the mounted chain gun, causing the front barrel to detach completely and fall into the charred sand, leaving him weaponless as he hung out the top of the jeep. He ducked low behind the armored shield that served as his only protection.

"I need a new weapon," he called into the cabin.

"What the hell happened to the chain gun?" Matt yelled back at him.

"There isn't a chain gun anymore," said James. "Now someone throw me a goddamn rifle before we all get killed, please."

Haley tossed a coil rifle up to him, which he promptly used to fire back at the pursuing car. His first couple shots fizzled off into the distance, but his last attempt called out with the satisfying ring of rending metal. The young rebel waited a moment and then popped up again, firing another burst. As he did, he watched Raphael shred the second gunner, then bisect the vehicle, causing it to spiral onto its side as its wounded driver lost control.

Hurtling past the wreckage of the gate, Matt brought the jeep screeching into the inner courtyard, followed closely by the Archangels. While the Crusaders were pressing their advantage outside the wall, within the reinforced courtyard the regime soldiers were having a better time of it thanks to their well dug in positions. Snipers fired out of the guard towers that rose up off of the wall, and machine gunners unloaded from atop the ramparts that ran along the entire length of the complex. Guards fired over parapets into the swarming masses as the once barren courtyard filled with bodies, blood, and burned out vehicles. Matt positioned the jeep as best he could to provide cover to the group as they exited the damaged transports. Michael did the same, except Raphael stayed in his turret nest, firing into the fray around him. The beast of a man continued shooting the large weapon, slaying guard after guard, until he heard the distinct click of a chain gun run dry.

He hopped out of the back end of the jeep and sprinted over towards the archway that the group had ducked into, attached to one of the numerous prison blocks housed within the facility. As he rounded the bend, Matt fired a barrage straight towards him, missing by a hair.

"You little bastard," said Raphael, reaching over his shoulder to unsling his coil rifle.

"You're welcome, you big bitch," replied Matt, nodding towards the fallen guard that had gone down right behind the hulking Crusader.

Raphael turned his head towards the corpse, grunted, then pushed past the rest of the group towards his brothers who were busy strapping breach charges to the doorframe. Matt, meanwhile, took down another two soldiers who were attempting to flank the besieged entry.

"Well holy shit!" Megan yelled over the nonstop blast of gunfire. "You're actually hitting something today."

"Hardy har har!" Matt yelled back, letting off another salvo. "I happen to be an excellent marksman. It just helps when the intel I'm getting isn't complete horseshit. If you put as much effort into intelligence gathering as you did insulting me, we'd have won the war years ago. Oh and by the way..." he started as an explosion went off in the nearby doorway. "Goddammit, I think you just shattered my eardrums," he yelled at the Archangels as he continued to fire out into the courtyard. Since they seemed not to hear him, he gave them the finger as he climbed through the newly blasted portal. "You guys are real assholes, you know that?" he continued, as they ran down the newly accessed hall. "And where the hell are we anyway?"

"If I brought us in where I think I did, we should be in District 3, Subsection D," Michael responded. "Dante is being held in D5 SA."

"OK, great, how are we going to find my dad?" said James.

"Dante first, he might know where your father is being held," said Michael, once again looking down to consult the floor plan he'd pulled up on his datacuff.

"Fine," replied James, eyeing the map. "Let's make this quick."

Michael nodded, pointing down the hall. "That's where we need to go. It should take us out near a central hub which we can use to access the other cellblocks."

The group ran past cage after cage, charging unopposed toward the wide double doors at the far end of the hallway.

"Where the hell are all the prisoners?" said Matt, turning to look through another set of black bars into an empty cell. "I thought this place would be bursting with detainees. This is nothing like the reports we've been getting for the last few months."

Dr. Reya nodded. "It's odd. It's almost as if they were evacuated before the battle began. Nightrick must've known we were coming well ahead of time."

Raphael motioned for silence as the group approached the final crossway of the cellblock. He held his hand up, halting the advance. A deep, strained breathing from around the bend pierced the silence. Quietly, he raised his coil rifle, then bolted around the corner, firing clean kill shots straight through the heads of two out of the three men waiting to ambush the rebels. The last surviving guard, a lanky young man who looked more apt to piss his pants than fight back, tried to lift his weapon towards the massive Archangel, but before he could manage it, he felt the metal round slide through his left elbow, like lightning striking a rod. He fumbled his rifle onto the ground in shock. Raphael smiled, then fired another shot off at the young soldier, sending this one tearing across his left thigh. The man doubled over in a cry of agony, clutching his shattered arm as if a bit of pressure might restore the bone. Raphael walked over to the fallen soldier and picked him up by the collar, throwing him effortlessly against the solid titanium door that blocked the advancing group from entering the central hub of the complex.

"Now," he said, unsheathing a long, sharp blade from his side as he stepped towards his wounded captive. "You're going to open that door for us with your biometrics, or I'm going to take what I need from you with this hunting knife and then slam what's left of you against the titanium until all that remains is a red paste smeared across the surface. Understand?"

The wounded man nodded feverishly, still sprawled out on the ground.

"Good," he replied, leaning over to hoist the fallen guard over his shoulder like another piece of equipment.

Once through the door, Michael took a moment to consult his map, and then led the group down a ways towards the eastside of the compound.

"Where the hell is everyone?" asked Matt. "Were those three men the only soldiers Nightrick had to spare?"

"Something is off," replied Dr. Reya, looking towards the half-dazed guard that was bleeding onto Raphael's shoulder. "This place should be crawling with guards. I can't imagine they sent them all out to the courtyard."

"They're...inner...," mumbled the captive.

"Come again?" said Dr. Reya, walking up to the young man.

His head rolled limply along Raphael's shoulder. "I said they're all defending the inner sanctum."

The physician nodded. "That makes sense I suppose, with Nightrick being here."

"Enough talk," said Raphael. "We're here."

He pulled the guard down in front of the access panel to District 5. The console scanned the young man's face, then chirped as the door slid open.

"Alright, everyone, keep your guard up," said Michael. "If they're going to try anything else, it'll be here."

The group entered the corridor with their weapons held high, slowly advancing from black-barred cell to black-barred cell. Half a mile down, they finally found their target. There before them, in a cage of steel, stood Dante, his head downturned, bathed in the rich yellow light that streamed in through the shielded window behind him.

He was an imposing figure, his presence far surpassing that of his physical size. His eyes blazed with a zealous fire, unbroken by his time in detention. It appeared that the Toxic Truth had met its match in him. His unkempt white hair hung freely from the sides of his head like loose yarn, giving him a wild look. It was hard to tell his exact age at a glance, as he neither appeared particularly old nor young. He wore a tattered white prisoner's uniform that was fraying along the seams. Despite his ragged appearance, the leader of the Crusaders looked to be in good health. He had the same toned physique that he had possessed when last Michael had laid eyes on him. The zealot waited a moment before raising his gaze to address his rescuers. "My faithful Archangels,

I knew it would only be a matter of time before you descended on this den of heathens to free me. And, Mira, so good to see you again. Hurry now, we must go before Dr. Nightrick realizes what's happening."

"Your holiness, it's good to see you in one piece," said Gabriel as he used a handheld on a nearby panel to open the cell. Despite being a literal cage, more appropriate for a dungeon than a prison, the cell still had the advanced electronic locking mechanisms that were standard for such facilities.

"Sir, we have one final order of business to attend to before we go," said Michael. "These four are CLF deserters here to free this one's father from Special Branch."

"Deserters?" replied Dante eyeing the group. "And who, pray tell, is this?" he asked, pointing at the wounded guard who had been set down next to the Archangels.

"He's some stupid son of a bitch who tried to get in between us and you," said Raphael.

"I see," replied Dante, reaching into Raphael's holster and pulling out his sidearm. He looked at the weapon for a moment, and then, in one clean motion, shot the guard execution style through the head. As the man slumped over, Raphael chuckled, Gabriel nodded, and Michael stood there expressionless. Of the Crusaders, only Dr. Reya looked upset about their leader's wanton brutality. The CLF

deserters, however, began to protest all at once before Dante raised the weapon at them.

"I'm afraid we won't be having any time to help
you lot. I think I'll save you and Dr. Nightrick the
trouble by putting you down now. There's no room
in this war for those who fight without righteousness
in their hearts."

Matt frowned. "More like self-righteousness, you
maniac. We help free you and this is how you thank
us?"

"I wouldn't expect a member of the CLF to understand the nuances of rectitude. Your soul is mud-
died and only I can make you pure again. Let the
vale of death wash you and cleanse you of your sins."

"Wait! Wait!" cried Michael. "I promised to help
them. They were instrumental in freeing you, your
holiness! They could still be of use to us!"

"A pleasant thought, but I'm afraid not, Michael.
Sinners are cast into the fire. I would have hoped
you had learned that long ago."

The moment that Dante averted his gaze to address his protesting soldier, Megan tried raising her
weapon to fire on him. Halfway up, Raphael's hand
was there to meet the barrel, forcing it back down.
He roughly pulled the coil rifle away from her before
she could try using it again. Noticing the commotion,
Dante raised his borrowed handgun at her, and as
he did, without thinking, Michael disarmed the man

in one swift motion. The rogue Archangel shoved Dante aside and laid a hard elbow into Raphael's sternum before the man could even react, causing him to double over as the air evacuated his lungs. Gabriel stood there for a second, unsure which of his brothers to assist. After a moment, he raced to restrain Michael, but as he did, Matt and James slammed into him, pinning him hard against the metallic bars and knocking him out cold. Dante scrambled across the floor towards Gabriel's fallen rifle.

"Run!" screamed Michael, turning to bolt back down the corridor. Everyone fled, except for Dr. Reya, who had leaned over to check on Raphael. Dante pushed up onto his feet and brought the rifle racing up. The group made it back through the door just in time for the zealot to let off the first clip.

"Your time is coming! You cannot escape the fire that awaits you!" he yelled as the ragged group continued running full speed down the hall, away from the district. As Dante lowered his weapon, Raphael managed to prop himself up on his elbow and reach for his own fallen rifle. He gazed over at his unconscious brother and moved to lift him.

"Leave him," said Dante.

"But, sir, he's just unconscious!" said Dr. Reya.

"I said leave him. We don't have time to be lugging around the helpless."

"He's my brother. He's coming with us," said Raphael, beginning to reach for his sibling again.

"A martyr's death awaits him. You will feast with your brother again in the Halls of Paradise. There's no time for him now though, we stand on the brink of victory. I have seen the end. Our way is forward. We must reach the inner sanctum before Dr. Nightrick manages to seal it off entirely."

"But, sir...," Raphael began to protest.

Dante raised his weapon and shot Gabriel in the head. Dr. Reya screamed in horror as the man convulsed in response to the kill shot.

"He died a hero, never forget that," said Dante, looking down at his last remaining Archangel. "Now onward to victory."

Raphael turned bright red, taking the shade of an enraged bull. The wild look in his eye ignited, then faded like a dying star casting out its light before going dark. As quickly as the fury had come on, it passed away with whatever remained of Raphael's sanity.

"He's at peace now, Raphael. Do not mourn the dead, my child, for their fight has ended. Ours, on the other hand, is just beginning. Now come. We have work to do."

⇒‡ ‡⇐

The rebels ran for what felt like miles before finally coming to a halt in front of another security door at the end of one of the complex's thousand hall-ways. Thick, projectile-resistant glass loomed over Megan's head as she ducked down near the access console. With Michael's help, she pulled the panel-ing off of the terminal and connected her datacuff to it with a thin wire, while Matt limped up behind them.

"Good God, I can't breathe," he huffed, leaning his forearm against the wall.

"How the hell did you manage to get into pro-gressively worse shape as the war has gone on, Matt?" Megan asked, looking up at him. "Most peo-ple fighting for their lives tend to get stronger. You, on the other hand, appear to be transforming into gelatin."

"Oh I don't know, Megan, maybe it has some-thing to do with being shot, stabbed, blown up, and beaten every other day. How can I stay in shape when the universe is constantly trying to kill me?"

She shrugged. "A treadmill?"

"Treadmills don't increase the ballistic armoring of your skin," he said, pulling the damp, blackish red cloth of his right pant leg aside. "That fucker clipped me on the way out of his cellblock. I didn't even real-ize I'd been hit until I felt my leg giving out a little ways back."

"Shit," said Michael. "That's just great, and Mira chose to stay with Dante. Let me give you a hand with that." He pulled a thin roll of cloth out of his rucksack along with an unmarked plastic bottle. After unscrewing the cap, he dabbed the cloth in the liquid and began meticulously cleaning the wound. "He did a little more than clip you," he said, pulling a clean section of cloth off of the roll. "I'd bet good money there's some metal in there right now. We'll tie it off for the moment and take care of it once we get the hell out of here."

"If we get the hell out of here," said Haley, looking around the corridor. "Where are we even?"

"I'm not actually one hundred percent sure," said Michael, pulling a knot into the fabric wrapped around Matt's leg. "We ran further into the complex though, so we're likely headed toward the inner sanctum. If Nightrick is interrogating your father, that's probably where he's holding him."

"Alright," said James. "And thanks for the help back there. Dante is out of his goddamn mind."

"I hate to admit it, but I'm starting to agree," said Michael. "Dante was never overflowing with mercy to begin with, but he was certainly more flexible before. He was opportunistic more so than he was dogmatically rigid. In the past he might have welcomed turncoats with open arms. Now apparently he executes them."

"We're not turncoats," replied Matt, wincing as Michael pulled another section of cloth firmly around his wounded thigh.

"Well, helping us free Dante seems to suggest that you are. Good luck explaining all of this to your superiors. They'll put all four of you up against a wall for what you've done here."

James nodded in agreement. "Fuck the CLF. We're independent operators now. I don't care what anyone's affiliation is anymore. It's all meaningless. Just words in the wind. All I know is that anyone who stands in between me and Dr. Karich is my enemy, and I'll put them down without a second thought."

Megan swiped another command across her datacuff and the heavy blast door that had been blocking their way slid aside. "We're in."

"Perfect timing," said Michael, pushing back onto his feet. "Matt's leg should be fine until we can finish up here."

Haley leaned over and picked up the coil rifle that she had propped up against the wall. "Good, then we need to keep moving. As soon as Dante and your friends make it out of here, our entire distraction is gone, and then we'll be all that's left standing against an army."

CHAPTER ELEVEN

Raphael stepped through the singed door-frame leading into the inner sanctum, firing relentlessly at the remaining sentries now writhing on the ground in agony. One by one they ceased their pathetic squirming, blank stares broadcasting from their once living faces. Dante swept into the room, pausing to peer through a window that looked out over one of the facility's countless interrogation chambers. Large machines with tubes and wires of all sizes running their duration surrounded a chair equipped with bindings. Next to the seat was a tall table upon which scalpels, pliers, and various other instruments rested. Dr. Reya crept in behind her two companions, trying her best to go unnoticed.

"Dreadful places," said Dante, more to himself than anyone else. "And yet, so much potential to do good with their technology. The Lord works in mysterious ways." He looked over at his physician, seeming to notice her for the first time since they'd left his prison block. "You know, when I first got here they tried desperately to reprogram me like they did to every other two-bit rebel leader they've captured since building this place. Day in and day out they'd use every trick in the book to brainwash me, but they could never do it. See, their techniques only work on the weak willed and the weak minded. I was able to fight back their advances because my faith was strong enough to shield my mind.

"When reprogramming failed, they decided that perhaps they could torture me into breaking and then try again. They assigned a distinctly sadistic doctor to use any means necessary to drive me over the edge. He flayed me, stabbed me, burned me, broke my body but never my spirit. Week after week, month after month, I endured his brutality, sustained only by the grace of the Lord. While I underwent their 'therapies', I received countless visions from the hereafter. I've seen the end of this war, Dr. Reya. A rebirth is coming, and it will herald death for the doctor and his army of slaves," he said, pulling back away from the window he had been transfixed on. He proceeded forward down the hall, pausing to read the plates on each door as he went.

"Sir, what exactly are we looking for?" asked Dr. Reya.

"First we're going to pay an old friend of mine a visit, and then we need to locate this facility's Induction chambers. They have records here that outline how to perform the procedure in exquisite detail."

She nodded. "I see. You mean to destroy this facility's capacity to carry out Induction."

"Destroy it? No, no, no, Doctor. I don't mean to destroy anything. I mean to use it."

The physician felt her stomach turn, but she didn't say another word. She just followed the zealot down the hall, keeping a safe distance from Raphael, as he lumbered closely behind his master. His blank face looked gaunter than it had just an hour earlier and he hadn't said a word since leaving Dante's cellblock.

"There it is!" exclaimed Dante, pausing in front of one of the numerous rooms that lined the long hall. "Raphael, if you'd be so kind…"

The Archangel slammed his giant black combat boot into the door, knocking the hardwood off of its hinges. The barricade crashed inward, opening the room to the trio.

"Thank you," said Dante, stepping over the fallen door into the office. He looked around the room, taking in the exquisite order with which every single item had been placed. There was a symmetry to the furniture that seemed almost obsessive in its execution. Two ferns on either side of the door, two chairs beside the lone, carefully centered desk, and two bookshelves pushed up against the walls across from each other, filled to the brim with a variety of thick-spined encyclopedias and medical texts, each one aligned perfectly with its neighbor. The lone occupant of the room let out a small squeak. Dante stared at the man quivering behind his desk for a moment before proceeding to sit down in one of the chairs adjacent. "Dr. Tellman, so good to see you again. Please, take a seat."

The man rose shakily, and sat back into his leather chair. His pasty skin was moist with perspiration, and the bald spot in the center of his head was highlighted by the damp hair surrounding it. As he adjusted his posture, he noticed Dante staring at the scalpel on his desk.

"Now there's a tool that I know you're familiar with," said the zealot, raising his eyes to the man.

"Please," started Dr. Tellman, shaking even worse than before. "I was just doing…"

He cut short his thought as Dante raised his hand at him, signaling silence.

"There's no need to grovel, Doctor. You aren't in any danger yet, I assure you. Quite the contrary really. You'll be coming with me. I have a good deal of work for you. I'm hoping you'll be up to the challenge."

"W... w ... w ... work?"

"Yes, Doctor. The Crusaders are branching out, and you'll get to play a starring role in our expansion. I know many people who would literally kill to be granted such a distinct honor."

"W... what would I be doing exactly?"

"In time, Doctor, in time. See, Dr. Reya, how eager our newest recruit is? That go-getter attitude will get you far with me, Tellman. Now come along, I'd like you to escort me to the Induction chambers if you'd be so kind."

"What for?"

"Again, Doctor, in due time," responded Dante, rising from his seat. "Raphael, if you would, make sure that the good doctor here doesn't fall behind."

As the brute of a man approached the pasty captive, the doctor let out an audible squeak and hurried over to the door to lead the group through the maze of crisscrossing hallways that comprised the inner sanctum.

"Step quickly, Doctor! You're doing the Lord's work now," said Dante through the twisted smile on his face.

A dull blue light glimmered through each pane of the reinforced glass that stretched the length of the hall. The cells in the inner sanctum were less like cages and more like suites. The corridor was lined with well furnished rooms containing everything that one could possibly desire. They had been built for captive high priority targets whom Dr. Nightrick deemed worthy of not suffering the indignity of being tossed into the actual prison that sat just a few blocks over. Mostly though, the rooms got used by high ranking Neuro Corp employees and government officers visiting the facility.

Dr. Karich sat there in one such suite, trying to figure out the source of the cacophony that he continued to hear. Explosions, gunfire, sirens, it sounded like a warzone, and it sounded like that warzone was moving towards him at an alarming speed. He stood up, continuing to stare out the mesh window. The sound of his cell door sliding open brought him back to the present moment. A brilliant green light rose up from the lone AI console sitting nearby.

"Your presence is requested by Dr. Nightrick," stated Turing. "Please allow the Shadow Guard to escort you to the Citadel."

A phalanx of soldiers flanked him as he walked out of the suite and dutifully made his way towards the stronghold that Nightrick used as his private chamber in the facility. The warriors surrounding him wore the signature black armor of Special Branch, each one masked in the same plated helmet that made them the faceless agents of destruction they were renowned to be. As the group entered Dr. Nightrick's accommodations, he stood up from behind his desk to greet them. "Omar, Central Intelligence has just informed me that your son is approaching this wing to try and free you as we speak. I hate to be the bearer of bad news, but he's insurmountably outnumbered."

"If you do anything to harm him, John, you mark my words that my last act on this planet will be to crush the air out of your lungs."

Nightrick walked to the other side of his desk. "I have no desire to harm him; I just want to speak with him. He's got the potential to do great things if he can free himself from the ideological shackles that bind him. The easiest way to avoid a violent confrontation here, obviously, would be for you to explain to your son the situation and convince him that it's in everyone's best interest to avoid any further fighting."

"Why would I help you?"

"Because you'll be burying your boy if you refuse to help me put a leash on him. I won't allow you people to further escalate an already unnecessary and brutal conflict because you want to take turns playing hero. If James works with me, together we can do great things. We can end this war and forge a new path forward for humanity, a path that will cast our light out to the farthest reaches of the galaxy. Your son is brilliant. I don't want to see him squander his talent and his life dying in a futile and useless war against progress. I wouldn't wish to deprive our species of everything that he's capable of. But he's young and he's reckless. As you're well aware, I was like that once too, but I saw the light in time to avoid destroying myself. I have a feeling that only you will stand a chance of talking any sense into him, and if you can't, I'll contain the situation without a second thought." A second alarm blared loudly over the still shrieking first. Nightrick tapped his datacuff, silencing the siren. "They're about two districts down. They'll be here shortly. I implore you to make the right decision. If you care about your son's future at all, you'll help me make sure that he has one."

⊰⊱

Haley stared down the hall at the final door standing between them and the cellblock that they were fighting their way toward. She pushed on, even though she felt like her body was getting ready to shut down. The prison was less of a complex and more of a city, exhaustingly large and horrendously well manned. Matt hobbled along beside her, wincing every so often but keeping a decent pace. As they bypassed the final door into the inner sanctum, the group came to a halt. There before them stood Dr. Karich, pacing outside of his now open cell.

"Dad," said James running towards him.

"How could you be so stupid, James? I taught you better than this," said Dr. Karich, embracing his son. "This is suicide. And you brought Haley along for this madness? This has to stop. Put your weapons down and Dr. Nightrick has agreed to spare all of you. He doesn't want to fight you, James, he wants to work with you. Your life doesn't have to end here."

James frowned. "Work with me? I'll never work with that tyrant. He's enslaving our entire species, why can't you see that? He alone is responsible for the deaths of millions. He shells civilians indiscriminately, tortures dissenters, enslaves the young, and sweeps aside the old. There'll be no peace until he's been removed from power."

"Removed by what, James? The five of you? He has an army at his disposal and unlimited resources. If you try to fight him here, he'll kill us all. I'm not going to let you throw your life away like this. It's meaningless."

"It's not your life to throw away, it's mine."

"And what about Haley? I imagine you two ran away so that you could be together. Getting yourselves killed here will have made that thoroughly pointless. If you end this now, I'm sure that we can convince Dr. Nightrick to give both of you a pass on Induction. I've known him for a long time, James, a lot longer than you. He can be a reasonable man, just don't push him any further."

"What about me?" said Haley, stepping forward. "We made our decision together and we're standing by it. If we don't fight Nightrick now, while we still can, soon there will be no one left to oppose him."

Dr. Karich shook his head. "There will be no one left to oppose him if you all die here because you're too proud to stop. Survive now, fight later. You kids don't know the first thing about war. You think this is a game? I've seen what comes from rebellion, and trust me, it's never what you hope it will be."

A burst of gunfire rang out in the block as Michael staggered to one knee. He pulled his hands back from his side, smeared in crimson. The group turned, reflexively raising their weapons as Dante and his ensemble approached from the adjacent access way.

"I hope I'm not interrupting this very touching reunion," said Dante, keeping his handgun trained on Michael. "It looks like you didn't need our help after all. I haven't been able to locate our old friend Dr. Nightrick yet. I don't suppose you've seen him?"

"Raphael," Michael groaned in agony, still clutching his side. "Where's Gabriel?" He didn't need a response to know what had happened. The shamed, infinitely sad look on his brother's face said more than any words ever would. "How could you?" he murmured in disbelief. "He was our little brother, our flesh and blood. He loved you, Raphael! He would have died for you!"

"I'm a soldier, Michael, same as you are, same as he was," said Raphael. "We all knew exactly what we were putting on the line when we joined the Crusaders."

Michael looked down at the ground. "Then both of my brothers are dead."

Dante sneered at him for a moment before lowering his pistol. "Well, I'd love to stay and chat but I have pressing business to attend to," he said, turning to continue down the cellblock towards Nightrick's chambers. "This seems more like a family matter anyway. Raphael, make sure that these traitors and blasphemers do not interrupt me ever again."

Before the massive Archangel could raise his coil rifle, Michael flew at his brother like lightning, blind to the physical pain that he had felt just moments before. He knocked the weapon away and grabbed onto his collar, trying with all his might to throw the giant. Raphael countered, sending the duo into a spinning grapple. They jostled, slamming each other against the walls, both locked in their final embrace. The giant finally managed to break the stalemate, slamming his head into his brother's so hard that he went blind for a moment. Michael

staggered backwards in a stupor, just barely dodging the flurry of swings being thrown at him as his
vision blurred back into focus. He fought with all his
might, but he was losing blood too fast to maintain
his strength. He took another desperate lunge at
Raphael, who simply snatched him out of the air as
if he was a plaything. The giant lowered him back to
the ground and brought his boot down through his
knee, crushing the leg backwards. Michael screamed
in agony as the bone gave way before the onslaught
of the black combat boot. Resisting the urge to pass
out, he propped himself up on his remaining knee,
grabbing hold of the nearby doorframe for support.

Raphael took a moment to regard his older
brother before kicking the gimped man square in
the chest, collapsing a number of his ribs and fling-
ing him back into the cell through the sheer force of
the blow. By the time he landed on the tiled apartment floor, Michael was so deep in shock that he
could barely even feel his imploded chest. It was all
he could do to draw enough oxygen into his body to
remain conscious.

The two Archangels were still too close to each
other to offer a clean shot to anyone else in the room.
Turning from his brother, Raphael drew his sidearm
in response to James's attempt to rush him, squeezing off the first shot with the effortless accuracy of
someone who treated their weapon like an extension

of their own arm. As James realized his mistake, he felt the impact of Dr. Karich's foot, knocking him into Matt.

Raphael fired another shot at the tumbling rebels, but failed to get a third off before being tackled by the doctor. Both men went careening into the cell onto Michael, who spit a large glob of blood up into the air as the duo landed on his battered chest. The moment the path was clear, Megan ran over to the room's exterior interface and quickly locked the cell door with her datacuff, causing the entry to slam shut as Raphael and Dr. Karich rose to their feet.

⊨╬╠⊨

The Archangel hammered blow after blow down onto his significantly older opponent, but the doctor managed to deflect all of them. Dr. Karich brought his knee up hard into Raphael's groin and turned, rolling the giant off of his hip. The Crusader pushed out of the spin and back onto his feet, albeit hunched a bit from the strike. He kicked for his opponent's knee to collapse it as he had his brother's, but the chemist was faster. The old man dodged sideways and swept up with his hand, forcing Raphael's leg past its natural elevation, sending the giant spiraling down hard onto the cell's surface.

The Archangel propped himself onto his hands and knees with a grunt. For the first time that day, he could feel a trickle of blood running down his chin. He shoved back onto his feet and studied his opponent for a moment, pacing the room without reengaging. Dr. Karich stared back, never breaking eye contact. The Archangel nodded, wiping away the blood on his face with the back of his hand. "Congratulations, old man. You're the first decent fight I've had all day."

Dr. Karich gave him a small smile. "I'm also the last decent fight you'll ever have, so enjoy it."

"We'll see," said Raphael, sweeping down on him again like a hurricane. The doctor blocked each blow, but he could feel his arms beginning to give way under the immense power of the beast trying to kill him.

James untangled himself from Matt, scrambling back onto his feet. The side of his chest felt bruised from the raw force behind his father's kick, but he ignored the pulsing pain as he ran to collect his weapon off the floor nearby. Haley and Matt were already at the cell door by the time James had gotten over to them.

"Megan, open the door," said Matt, giving her a nasty look. "We don't have time for this shit."

She shook her head. "We can't risk Raphael escaping. He's got enough chlorine gas on him to flood the entire cellblock with it."

"I'm armed, for God's sake, open the fucking door!" Matt yelled at her. She backed away, never letting her gaze wander from Michael's broken body. As the argument continued, James's eyes were locked squarely on his embattled father.

In the cell, Dr. Karich continued to keep Raphael at bay, but he could tell that he was no match for the seasoned Crusader. He looked out on James, and realized that the second the boy managed to get the cell door open again, the now cornered Archangel would unleash his chemical arsenal, turning the entire sector into a vapor holocaust. He smiled at his son one last time, then slipped his fingers through two of the metal rings dangling off of Raphael's vest and pulled. The Archangel tried to stop the old man, but he was too slow. As the first ring cleared the green canister that it had adorned, a stream of pressurized gas poured into the room.

"DAD!" screamed James, running over to the cell door as Raphael and Dr. Karich stopped fighting each other and started fighting for air in the quickly filling chamber. He pounded his fist against the glass, then stepped back and unloaded his rifle into the sheet, which cracked, but held.

"Open the door! Open the ventilation ducts in the room, Megan! Hurry!" he said, tossing his empty rifle aside with a wild look on his face.

"I can't. If Raphael survives, then everyone here dies. Your father knew what he was doing."

James rushed at her with blood in his eyes, drawing his sidearm and raising it to her head. "Open the fucking door now or you'll be taking the same trip as everyone in that room." He could hear his father gasping for air. He glanced sideways and saw the men pressed against the glass, instinctively trying to free themselves. As he caught his son's eye, Dr. Karich stopped struggling and pressed his middle finger, forefinger, and thumb up against the glass in the form of an upside down triangle. James watched his father reaching out towards him in his final moments, trying still to save his son.

"James!" cried out Haley, causing him to turn towards her. "Don't! It's not what he would want!"

As he turned his attention momentarily towards his girlfriend, Matt tried to make a move. He sprinted forward as best he could, but his wounded leg slowed him. James threw a hard knee into his chest, sending him reeling backward. "One more step, Matt, and she's gone. Now open the door, Megan, or I'll open you."

"I'm so sorry, James. I know how hard this is for you but I can't…" The slug knocked her head back, lifting her just slightly off of her feet. James grabbed her wrist with his free hand as her lifeless body slumped over against the wall. Matt let out a cry of rage and rushed at him once again, but couldn't move fast enough. James leveled the pistol and fired another shot clean through his friend's already damaged right leg. Matt collapsed onto the floor in an erratic spasm, blacking out in an ever growing pool of his own blood.

"JAMES!" screamed Haley in disbelief. "You… you…"

"Did what had to be done," he responded with an angry confidence that sent a shiver through her whole body. He tossed the depleted pistol aside and tapped the datacuff attached to the deceased woman's wrist, turning on the ventilation shafts and rapidly sucking the poisonous cloud from the room, lifting the vale of death. James touched the display one more time, opening the door to the cell, before tossing Megan's limp arm aside like a piece of trash. He rushed into the room, turning Dr. Karich over onto his back. The master chemist had closed his eyes before dying, but the greenish-yellow skin on his face was blistered and disfigured. The young rebel let out a cry of fury as he held his father's head. For the second time in his life, he faced the agony of being orphaned. He looked through the pane of glass at Haley, who had rushed over to Megan. A large part of the dead woman's skull had detached as a result of the near pointblank shot, and it hung loosely as Haley lifted her to check her condition.

"You killed her…" she started in disbelief. "She was your friend, James…you… you killed her…"

"She killed my father," he bit back in blistering rage. His red eyes turned on her in disgust. "The bitch killed my father. She's lucky that she got the quick death she did."

"And Matt," she continued, standing up and approaching the grievously wounded CLF agent. "He needs medical attention or he's going to bleed out. What have you done?"

"They killed him, Haley. I warned them both never to threaten the safety of my family again," he gasped out, trying hard not to let his anger turn against her. "Whose side are you on? He loved you like a daughter, Haley. Fuck Megan and Matt. All we have left in this world now is each other."

"You know that I loved him too, but he never would have wanted this. If all we have left is each other, then I have nothing left at all."

James gently set his father's head back down against the cool tile and stood up to approach her. As he neared the door, the heavy metal slammed shut again, locking him in the chamber.

"What the hell?" he said, slamming his fist against the door. One final shot rang out in the cellblock. He looked out at Haley as she staggered forward a step or two before collapsing onto the ground next to Matt. Dr. Nightrick walked into view of the chamber, holding a small handgun at his side. The Shadow Guard stood nearby, maintaining a respectable distance.

"She's fine, James, just unconscious," said the doctor, bending over to check her pulse. He paused before standing back up, eyes locked on his old friend's corpse. "What a mess. I'm sorry about what happened to your father. Omar Karich was one of the greatest men that I've ever known, and I'm proud to have called him a friend once. His loss is a scar that this nation will bear until its twilight. Your father was a wise man, James, wise enough to see how fruitless all of this fighting is, and yet still he paid the ultimate price. This is the legacy that the Crusaders leave everywhere they go: carnage. That coward Dante ran off the second he realized that he's only strong against unarmed civilians."

"He died because of you!" James spat back at the doctor, turning the full fury of his gaze onto him. "Because you kidnapped him! He only said what he did to try and save me."

"Omar died because you helped to free a mentally unstable convict. Do not allow his sacrifice to be meaningless, James. Join me and we can avenge your friends and family. Together we can crush these uprisings and carry our species forward into the Golden Age of Man. This senseless violence has to stop. It's taking too many lives. It's wearing our people down, James. It's degrading our empire, and for what? Soon all that will be left to fight for is dirt and ash. Think what we could accomplish if we laid down our arms and worked side by side. We could rebuild our lost cities, heal our wounded, and rise again, stronger than before. You've seen firsthand the progress of the IMMORTAL Initiative. By combining our talents we could give mankind eternal life, and with it, build an empire unconfined by the terrestrial boundaries that shackled our forbearers. We could conquer the stars and finish fulfilling the destiny of Man."

"You're deluded," said James, shaking his head lightly. "Everything you touch withers. You're no different than Dante, you just worship a different god. If you touch one hair on Haley's head, I'll skin you alive."

"I've no intention of harming my guest here, James. I just need to hold onto her until you've allowed reason to seep into that seemingly thick skull of yours. It's obvious that your grief is blinding you, so I'll give you time to mourn before demanding a choice. Just remember that your father saw the wisdom in unity, and I'm hoping that in time you will as well. I'm leaving now, and she's coming with me. If you want her back, we'll be at the Atria Plant. This cell door will open in one hour's time. I've commanded the remnant here to allow you to leave unmolested. Think very carefully about the future that you want to help create, James. I'll see you soon, I'm sure," said Nightrick, lifting his captive up off the ground and beginning to walk away.

"Nightrick," James said, causing the doctor to look back. "I will kill you for this."

"I wouldn't get my hopes up if I were you."

And with that, the doctor left.

CHAPTER TWELVE

J ames collapsed into the sand again, this time unsure of whether or not he would be able to get
back up. He crawled along, clawing futilely at the
fickle ground as the last bit of moisture dripped
out of his body onto the golden dune beneath him.
Raising his gaze up to the cloudless sky, he squinted
at the blinding sun that was now in full retreat to the
west. He'd been aimlessly trudging through the desert for at least two hours now, and it was beginning
to take its toll. While Nightrick had made it abun-
dantly clear before departing the Toxic Truth that
he wanted James let go, the sadists left to carry out
those orders had interpreted them in a very broad
way. Certainly they had let him go, but at no point
had the doctor specified what exactly the prisoner

was allowed to take with him. The guards stripped his gear from him and threw him out into the brutal Brukan Desert. He rolled over onto his back and shut his eyes as the searing hot sand continued to burn his body. His skin felt thoroughly cooked, bright red, like a piece of iron drawn forth from a forge. On top of that, the dull, throbbing pain in chest was beginning to sharpen. It would be over soon enough. He tried to turn back over, but couldn't quite muster the strength. Giving up, he closed his eyes and stopped squirming, letting the heat take him. Right as he grew still, he heard a soft sound approaching from the horizon. As the noise grew louder and louder, James opened his eyes again and squinted out over the boundless, rolling terrain. There in the distance, approaching quickly, he spotted a small convoy of black jeeps headed right for him. He consumed what strength he had left hobbling into an upward stance. No doubt a quick execution beat the protracted end he was facing there in the heat. The young rebel did his best to stand upright, so that he could face death with some level of dignity. As the vehicle's occupants drove into view, his heart sank again.

"Mr. Mercer, it appears that there's no avoiding you today," said Dante as he jumped out of the jeep and into the warm sand. "I take it that if you're here, my faithful servant met his end in Charon. Dr. Reya here was just telling me about you and your friends. Hard to believe that I've lost all three of my Archangels in one day thanks to you four. I must say though, that you survived this long is nothing short of a miracle. And for us to find you on our last pass through the desert? I'm beginning to feel that our destinies must be intertwined. Perhaps the Lord wills that I use you as a tool."

At that point, James was too weak to even utter a response. He just stood there shaking as his muscles begged to give out, wishing with all his might that he could somehow find the strength to kill Dante.

"You seem resourceful enough, and it's obvious that Dr. Nightrick wants you for some reason or he'd have killed you when he had the chance," continued Dante. "The man is unfeeling, but hardly cruel. I doubt he knows that you've been cast out into the desert. I take it you're a chemist?"

James gave a shallow nod in response. He could barely look on Dante as the blinding sun set against his figure, framing him in an otherworldly aura.

"Perhaps you would care to join me then? After all, our common enemy awaits us, and I could always use another talented chemist for what's to come."

James nodded his head meekly in agreement.

"Excellent," said Dante, turning towards one of the men sitting in the jeep behind him. "Get him some water and help him in. It's time we evacuate the desert." He turned back towards his new chemist. "A heathen converted in the wasteland. I think I'll call you Saul. You will be my instrument, and with you I will spread the faith far and wide."

⚔

James floated through the void, looking for the dancing flames of Haley somewhere off in the distance, but no matter which direction he swiveled his head, only darkness met his gaze. Her light had gone out at last. He swam farther into the blackness, then felt himself begin to fall, like a rock hurtled off of a mountain. Down and down he went, crashing onto a dry, cracked surface. He looked around at the sundered terrain, bathed in a purplish light from someone unseen source. The ground beneath him looked like a lakebed, long since vaporized.

"Hello?" he called into the ethereal vapor around him.

"Hello, James," said Megan, walking out of the fog. Behind her hobbled Matt, his leg torn asunder and his lips sewn shut.

"You're...you're alive," he said, backing away from the two.

"No, James. You saw to that. Remember?" she said, reaching up and lacing her fingers through the skin and bone at the top of her skull. She pulled the flap aside, and it fell loosely down, connected only by the untorn skin at the bottom.

"I'm…I'm sorry. I had to; you didn't give me any choice. I had to save my father."

Megan glided towards him. "You killed us, James, and you killed Haley too."

"No…," he said, backing up even further. "She's still alive. Dr. Nightrick has her at the Atria Plant. It's not too late to save her."

"But who will save her from you?" asked Megan, her voice like a hollow echo. "You've been with the Crusaders for weeks, and still nothing. You'll never see Haley again."

He stopped moving as he felt the dry ground begin to wet beneath him, gaining a muddy texture. "I will. They've been having me produce Induction-grade chemicals. They'll need more equipment to use the massive stockpiles. They have to attack the Atria Plant or the Rikon Plant, and the Atria is larger. It's the only place on Earth where they could hope to get enough equipment to use it all. It's not too late."

"Oh, but it is," said Megan. "Look around you, James. Even the Crusaders are using Induction now. The people have forgotten what they're fighting for. The good are always the first to die in war. All that survives is that which can…the cruel, the treacherous, and the willful. You're alone now, James, and you always will be."

He tried to run, but the mud had gotten too thick. He couldn't even pull his leg free anymore. Slowly, he sank into the bottomless sludge. Matt hobbled over to the pit, making a horrible sound, as if he was trying to speak without the ability to do so anymore.

"What? What's he saying?" cried James, sinking ever deeper into the muck.

"Failure," replied Megan, echoing into the boundless fog. "*Failure. Failure. Failure.*"

The boy looked out on the two figures floating above him, and then the mud overtook him. He tried flailing as his lungs filled, but to no avail.

James shot upright on the lumpy mattress he'd been given, woken by the pounding against his door. He sat there, heart racing, as the sound of the un-oiled doorknob turning echoed off the dank walls of the cellar he called a bedroom. Two militants stood in the doorway, coil rifles slung over their shoulders. Black silk cloth hung loosely from the Crusaders, covering them from head to toe, with only a thin slit for their eyes.

"Get up," said one of the men. "It's time."

"Time," said James, wiping away a bead of sweat from his damp forehead. "Time for what?"

The Crusaders didn't bother with a response. They just grabbed the young rebel and forced him onto his feet, marching him out of his chamber and down, towards the laboratories further below ground. When they reached their destination, the men nodded towards the plain metal door. As James entered the chamber, followed close behind by his escorts, he found a man strapped to an operating table in the middle of the room, sweating profusely and shaking in terror, struggling against his restraints to free himself.

"Good evening, Saul," said Dante, patting him on the back. "Tonight you will truly become one of us." He gestured at the two men standing in the doorway. "Strap him down."

"Wait wha…" started James as they roughly seized him up and shoved him down onto the table adjacent to the occupied gurney. He tried to shove the soldiers off, but they were simply too strong for him. He squirmed as they pulled the restraints around his arms and legs, binding him to the table.

"Well, now that that unpleasantness is out of the way, I believe we can begin," said Dante, eyeing the two unwilling patients. "Brothers and sisters, welcome. You should be honored to be a part of what transpires here this evening, for tonight we take the first step into a new age of revelation."

The first man's eyes widened in horror while James looked on in fury. Both victims began flailing even harder, trying to break the straps that bound them.

"These men are an abomination before our Lord," continued Dante. "They have served the forces of evil faithfully and they deserve none of our mercy. But despite their grievous crimes, the chalice of our Lord's kindness never runs dry. Tonight we will turn our enemy's weapon against them. Tonight we will begin winning converts through the very means that they have used to enslave us. Dr. Reya, prepare Dr. Tellman and our dear friend Saul for Induction."

The group of Crusaders stood there for a moment as a heavy silence settled over the room.

"Dante, Dante, please!" pleaded Dr. Tellman. "I told you everything you asked! I helped you make this possible! Let me continue my work for you! I swear my loyalty to you will be unwavering."

Dante raised his hand, silencing the man. "Oh, Dr. Tellman, I know all about your loyalty. Trust me when I say that shortly, your allegiance will be as real as the fear you feel now."

"Please! PLEASE!" screamed Tellman, jerking like a fish out of water.

"Someone muffle the good doctor. I would hate for him to strain his voice so shortly before being reborn."

One of the techs in the room carried out the order, gagging the raving captive with a dirty rag. Everyone else in the chamber just stood there, struggling with the wave of cognitive dissonance that was washing over them.

"Dante," said James, his fury quickly turning into desperation. "Dante, listen. If you Induct me, I'll be less effective as a chemist. I'm no good to you like that."

"Unfortunately, Saul, you and Dr. Tellman here have yet to take up the faith. Once you have, I'm sure you'll still serve some purpose. If it turns out to be cannon fodder for the more pure among our ranks, so be it."

"God damn you, Dante, you're a fucking snake," said James, now thrashing against his restraints as hard as Dr. Tellman. "You won't get away with this."

"Oh, I think I will, Saul. You don't seem to understand the simple truth of the matter; you belong to me. You're my property and I'll do with you as I please," he replied before turning back towards the still unmoving crew.

"Sir, you can't seriously mean to go through with this," said Dr. Reya, trying her best to keep her voice steady. "What about free will? A forced conversion is no conversion at all. We've sent thousands of men to their graves with the belief that they were dying to prevent this very process from occurring. It's disrespectful of our dead to even consider carrying it out."

Dante regarded her for a moment. "We're saving these men's souls, Doctor. Surely you don't oppose offering them eternal life? These men used their free will to make the wrong decisions, and now we are using ours to save them. It's corrective therapy for a damaged soul. Can there be a greater victory?"

"But who are we even binding them to? Why bother?" asked another member of the assembled.

"Why, we're binding them to the Lord of course," replied Dante. "They will spend the rest of their lives loving and serving our master, even if it is in a slightly different manner than we do. Their devotion will be as real as our own. They will be the first soldiers in our army of converts which we will use to break the power of those who would stand against us."

Though the assembled still looked rather uncomfortable, the response got them moving again. The technicians set to work preparing the chemical cocktails that would be needed for the procedure, trying all the while to ignore the muffled pleas of the men behind him. Once the rest of the machinery was set up, Dr. Reya hooked the final nodes into Dr. Tellman's skull as another chemist poured the necessary chemicals into the metallic tubes that lingered just above their unwilling patient. The balding man tried squirming, but his restraints had been tightened and he was held firmly in place. All he could do was look up helplessly and wait. James watched as Dr. Reya checked off Dr. Tellman's setup and moved over towards him to begin inserting the nodes into his own skull.

"Wait! Dante, hear me out!" said James. "I have a weapon that could help you win the war, but if you Induct me, I might forget how to make it."

Dante frowned. "I highly doubt that you have a super weapon hiding in your head, Saul. Now be quiet or I'll have you gagged like Tellman."

"It's a hypervolatilizer! It vaporizes liquids at unprecedented rates. It can also suspend heavier chemicals within the vapor. You could use it as a chemical weapon."

"I think I'll pass. We have plenty of chemical weapons already, and trust me when I say that they work just fine as is. Now get on with it, Dr. Reya, before I lose my patience."

She hesitated for a moment before picking up the syringe-laden tube and moving back towards James.

"If you dumped it into the chemical cocktails that you're using here, you could use it to Induct people via gas attacks," said James, trying to move his head away from the needle that Dr. Reya was reluctantly approaching him with.

"Wait," said Dante, signaling for the physician to step back. "Would that be possible, Doctor? Could Induction be carried out with gas if the chemicals were suspended?"

"Frankly, I have no idea," she replied. "The targets would have to be primed with neural mapping beforehand, or we'd have to find a way to guide the process chemically, but I suppose it's possible. No one has ever been able to try it, so who knows. Until now there hasn't been a way to vaporize these chemicals without causing them to lose their integrity. If what James says is true, it just might work."

James leaned forward as best he could. "The hypervolatilizer could stabilize and vaporize blood, let alone Induction-grade chemicals. I can't tell you whether the bindings will stick without proper neural mappings, but I can tell you that if they do, you'll be able to Induct entire cities in a single stroke. Think of the potential. If you Induct me, then you risk losing the formula as a result of turnover sickness. Don't lose thousands of converts trying to win one."

Dr. Reya nodded. "That's true, sir. There's a chance that he'll forget how to make the product if we Induct him. It's not unheard of to lose small fragments of memory during the process."

Dante stared down at James for a long moment. "Then release him."

As Dr. Reya undid the young rebel's straps, he clambered up and slid against the wall, shaking and clutching his seizing chest.

"We'll see if your compound will be of any use to us, Saul," said Dante. "If it isn't, you'll be back here soon enough."

James nodded, trying to recompose himself. Dante turned towards the raving Dr. Tellman, waving the techs back to the occupied gurney.

"Some would call this poetic justice," said Dante, looking down on his captive. "Today you are born again."

He signaled Dr. Reya, who promptly initiated the procedure. The prisoner closed his eyes tightly as the machines whined to life. When he finally opened them again, James found a pair of sickening, glazed brown pupils staring back. A short time ago it might have been enough to make him ill, but now he felt nothing looking back at the man. He just gazed deep into the brown glaze.

⇥⊹⊹⇤

James looked down the empty concrete hallway before rapping twice on the wooden door in front of him. Dim, artificial light shone down from the hanging fixture above, illuminating the complex buried deep beneath the earth. He waited a moment before raising his hand to knock again. As he did, the door opened.

"Hey, come in," said Dr. Reya.

James walked into the apartment and took a look around. A modest couch and coffee table sat against the wall. There was a bed was pushed up into the left corner of the main room and a small kitchenette sat off in the other corner. A modest bathroom was the only other chamber separated from the large one by a door, just before the bedframe.

"Wow, nice place," he said, walking in a little further. "Looks like you've got a lot of room here. They gave me a broom closet, but if there's anything I've gotten used to, it's living out of a closet. Looks like they even gave you a bathroom. You know what they gave me? A chamber pot. It's like I traveled back in time three hundred years."

She smiled. "Could be worse."

"Oh I don't doubt it," he replied, taking a seat on the couch.

Dr. Reya sat down across from him on a rather frayed, felt chair. She poured two cups of tea out of the pot that she'd set on the coffee table, then slid one across to James.

"So I performed another Induction today," she started, staring ahead for a moment before proceeding. "Another captured rebel. This one was from the Free Thought Brigade. He cried as I set up the final nodes, begging for mercy just like they all do. What the poor fool didn't understand was that Induction is mercy compared to how Dante usually handles prisoners. I've seen men shot in cold blood, beheaded, hell, even burned in cages, all while that maniac pontificates to the cameras."

"I remember seeing the videos online when I was younger. Those images never leave you, do they? They become a part of you, a dark cloud that follows you around for the rest of your life."

"That they do," she said with a distant tone.

James shifted in his seat a touch. "I thought I might end up back on the table today myself. Dante wasn't happy when he found out that I can't create the hypervolatilizer without the thermal stability of the Karrion catalyst. I assured him that Neuro Corp would have tons of it at the Atria Plant, but I think he's still considering just binding me and being done with it. At least I won't end up in one of his home movies now that he's mellowed with age."

"Believe it or not, he still makes the damn things, only now we're Inducting people on them instead of murdering them," she said, pausing to take a sip of her tea. "If you ask me, the people he murdered were better off than the people he bound. The newly Inducted have a lot of suffering to look forward to before they finally get to die. It won't be long until they're starving along with everyone else here. And it's not like there's not enough money to feed everyone, Dante just refuses to use any of it on food. You wouldn't believe how much we spend on production value for those little propaganda pieces. It's mad, but then again, everything is mad anymore."

James nodded.

"This group is a twisted caricature of what it once was," she continued. "In the beginning of the war, we were led by a man named Richard Crane. He detested violence and did his best to avoid it. Though we were the first group to take up arms against Dr. Nightrick, it was a matter of survival at that point, not desire. We couldn't just let Special Branch silence us, especially when they were defending a system of oppression unlike any the world has ever known. After the war started, Crane only lasted a year before they captured him. Special Branch made a very public showing of his execution, and from there things spiraled out of control fast. Dante rose up from obscurity, propelled by a fringe element of radicals that helped him to purge the group of those who opposed him. He slaughtered hundreds of his own people to secure his reign. And it wasn't just them, but their families too, men, women, and children, with no regard for the innocent.

"After a while, everyone remaining learned to just obey and keep their opinions to themselves. To be honest with you, when I first heard that Dante had been captured a year ago, I broke down in tears. I thought that maybe there would finally be a way out of this hellhole for everyone, but I under-estimated how deep his roots were here. Had the Archangels been detained with him we might have been free, but with them helping to enforce his will, things were virtually the same as they had always been: hopeless. During the interim, one of the high councilors, Donatello Carisnio, or as he's more com-monly known, the Templar Knight, ruled in Dante's stead. Turns out that he's as big of a bastard as our beloved prophet, if not worse. The only bright side to Dante being freed is that the Templar took off with his own entourage, apparently unwilling to give up power. Part of me hopes that he comes back one day and we just finish destroying each other. All I do anymore is wait for the end, praying that we're not the ones who win the war."

"How was Dante captured in the first place?" asked James, taking a moment to glance down at his newly returned datacuff as it chirped lightly to her-ald the start of another hour. "I'd of thought that they would just kill him and be done with it."

She shrugged. "I guess they learned their lesson from Crane's execution. There's always a greater evil lurking just behind the one you can see. Dante was captured in our botched attempt to blow up the Rikon Plant. We rolled enough explosives into the area to level not just the factory, but the entire surrounding city. If we had succeeded, hundreds of thousands of people would have died. Lucky for them, Dante decided to make another one of his little propaganda films before actually obliterating the area. He tries really hard to paint himself as some warrior of the faith, but on that particular day he couldn't get out of the blast radius fast enough and he ended up getting captured by General Joseph Bismuth and his army. See, Dante is happy to make martyrs out of others, but he'll never sacrifice his own precious life. In the end, the explosives were disarmed, Dante was carted off to the Toxic Truth, and we lost hundreds of people fighting an absolutely unwinnable battle. Doesn't make for a great propaganda piece, does it?"

"No, no it doesn't. And that sounds about right. He might be crazy, but he's not suicidal," said James, taking a long sip of his now lukewarm tea. "He fancies himself a prophet, I wonder if he knows how this all ends."

"It doesn't take a prophet or the gift of clairvoyance to know how this war will end," she said, shaking her head lightly. "It ends with ash and bone."

CHAPTER THIRTEEN

D r. Nightrick paused in front of the makeshift living quarters that had been set up in the Atria Plant. He knocked twice on the oak door that led into the suite, waiting a moment before entering. Haley looked up from the book that she had been engrossed in to acknowledge the intrusion. She stared at the man before her, keeping her expression carefully veiled.

"Awfully quiet today, Ms. Hall," said Nightrick. "Has your curiosity left you finally?"

"There's no point asking you anything if I never get a straight answer anyway. I don't even know why you bother coming up here. Doesn't conquering the world require your time more than these pointless talks we have?"

"In most cases, yes it would," he replied, stepping farther into the room. "But seeing as I haven't seen you since your last little getaway attempt, today I thought I'd stop by and ensure you understand that the next time you break out of this perfectly nice room I've given you, I'll be throwing you into a cage like the one you found Dante in. Don't make this harder on yourself than it has to be."

Haley brushed a strand of her auburn hair out of her face. "I wouldn't be able to get free so often if your people weren't so careless and stupid."

Nightrick sighed. "You fashioned a piece of cloth into a garrote and nearly strangled an unarmed kitchen boy to death the first time, and the second time you feigned a seizure then used a crudely crafted shank to kidnap a paramedic and make your way down to the distribution warehouse. Those aren't instances of carelessness or stupidity; they're instances of you taking advantage of my mercy. Now I suppose you could make the argument that mercy is indistinguishable from stupidity, but what is true power without the occasional kindness?"

"Yes, what a benevolent god you are. Maybe next you can tell me all about how your kindness and mercy led into the civil war that you're now losing?"

"Do you know why I've done the things I've done, Ms. Hall? When you look at Induction you see a world enslaved, but when I look at it, I see a world reestablishing balance. I see a world returning to the principles that gave our species power in the first place. Humans, in general, are naturally deficient creatures. For most of our existence, natural selection has worked to cleanse the weak, the undeserving, and the sub-virile from progressive generations, thus strengthening our genetic pool by forcing us to endure the crucible of evolution. But time, fate, and technology have made us weak. As we moved forward, we were able to cast a progressively wider shield around those of our kind who would otherwise have been rooted out, killing natural selection in the process. While it wasn't exactly a cataclysmic change for humanity, it was a turning point for us. We had, in the name of civilization, once again defied the will of nature. This time, however, our defiance came at a price."

"And so your solution to this made up problem of yours is to use a global eugenics program to destroy the weak. How noble of you."

He shook his head. "Not at all, you misunderstand me entirely, Ms. Hall. I'm not suggesting that protecting the weaker of our kind was a mistake. The power and responsibility to defend the defenseless is one of the hallmark traits of civilization. Mercy, in fact, is the only quality that separates us from other apex predators. What I'm saying is that with Induction, we can make all people better through careful and well planned pairing. There's a place for every person in the future that I've worked so hard to create. We need workhorses as much as we need scientists. A world full of intellectuals would be as useless as a world without them. I'm unlocking the true potential of our species by controlling one of nature's own tools."

"And the only price tag on your new world is freedom."

"You think you're free?" he responded, regarding her carefully for a moment. "See, that's the problem, I think. Those of you who would shed blood in the name of stopping me believe that doing so would somehow make the world free. Did you choose the conditions of your birth? Then you're a slave to fate. Did you choose the physical laws that bind you? Then you're a slave to nature. Did you choose to fall in love? Then you're a slave to hormones. Do you choose to digest your food? Then you're a slave to metabolism.

"Freedom is an illusion. It's a story that you all tell yourselves so that you can justify the terrible things you've done in the name of stopping me. I never wanted a war, I wanted a new world. I was born a builder, not a destroyer, and yet you've all managed to make me both. Life is one giant chemical reaction, and all I've done is manipulate the reactants in order to increase the yield of humanity's potential. In time, people with your way of thinking will come around, or I will bring them around with force. I don't even think you terrorists actually understand what Induction does. It's not mind control, Ms. Hall, it's just a slight alteration to your personality. It stabilizes the mind, bringing peace to the patient, lowering their violent tendencies, and even giving purpose to those who would otherwise feel like society had cast them aside. Induction is the great equalizer and the great stabilizer of our generation. After undergoing the procedure, the individual is still capable of thinking independently and acting exactly like they had before. You like the same foods still, enjoy the same movies, and are passionate about the same things as you were before undergoing the therapy. You're no different afterwards, save the fact that you're permanently and effortlessly in love with someone who loves you back. It's a gift really."

"You actually believe that freedom is an illusion, Nightrick? You think Induction is a gift? I bet if you were the one being dragged into one of your own Induction chambers you'd consider it to be a lot more tangible than you do when you're pontificating to a prisoner."

"Perhaps you're right about that, Ms. Hall. Maybe I would think differently if I was the one being Inducted. But that's a bit irrelevant really.

Hypocritical of me?" He shrugged. "I suppose it is. But at the end of the day, anyone who says they're not a hypocrite in some way or another is lying."

"Justify it however you want, all things end in time. Frankly, I don't know how regret doesn't consume you. You think you've laid the foundation for some infinite empire, but you're just a tiny man on a tiny planet with a tiny understanding of the universe. You may kill me and you may win a few battles, but you'll never douse the fire that you've ignited with words or weapons. Only your blood can extinguish the inferno, and soon enough it will. When they drag you out into the streets and execute you for all of your crimes against humanity, remember that it was you playing god that led to your collapse. Your ego is going to be your downfall, Nightrick."

"Guilt is for the self-righteous. If I die fighting this war, so be it, but I guarantee you that if I do, this country will burn until the sand turns to glass, and every man, woman, and child left on this planet will know that a pack of rabid dogs denied mankind its golden age."

"It's not your country to burn, Nightrick. What gives you the right to rule a nation that doesn't want you?"

He crossed his arms. "If the people didn't want me, I would have been dead a long time ago. They've made their choice."

Haley turned her gaze away from him and back to her book.

"Well, I'll leave you for now, Ms. Hall, to think about what we've discussed. I hope in time that you'll come around to my way of thinking."

And with that, Nightrick left the room.

———✦✦———

James stepped out of the dining hall after finishing another tasteless meal of greyish goop. The Crusaders spared no expense when it came to obtaining advanced weapon systems, but when it came time to feed their own people, the budget would suddenly run dry. Living conditions in the facility were just slightly above full on destitution. The only thing that kept morale from completely depleting was the faith that the average person there had in the next life. They might be poor now, but to face the trials and tribulations before them with courage would mean eternal glory in the hereafter. James walked along the concrete trail that snaked throughout the sprawling complex, brushing his hand against the thin groove in the wall. He turned at the sound of footsteps approaching from behind.

"Good evening, James," said Dr. Reya, speaking a bit softer than usual. "Would you care to join me for a drink?"

He nodded, following her back to her room in silence. Once behind the latched door, she retrieved an old bottle of bourbon from inside a makeshift cove in the wall and poured two generous portions into the glass cups she'd set on the countertop.

"Here you go," she said, handing one of the drinks to her guest as he sat down on the couch up against the wall. "Enjoy."

"Wow, where the hell did you get this?" he asked, holding the reddish brown liquid up to the light for a closer look. "Alcohol is a death sentence around here, I thought."

She smiled, sitting down in the chair across from him. "As are all things worthwhile. You know, in the beginning we didn't have to hide our vices and scurry around like rats. Richard Crane had his faults, sure, but he was a damn good leader. He was a fair man for a fairer time. Now, even the angels act like demons. I'm starting to think that there's no room left in heaven. All that's left to us is hell, and the graveyard that we slaughter each other for control over. Coren isn't a country, it's a crypt. I think if Richard were still here, he would regret ever having started this death cult." She took a sip of the liquid, cringing ever so slightly as she did. "It's always the first taste of bourbon that's the most brutal. It has a fire to it that can be vicious, but appealing at the same time. I think that's what this whole conflict has become really. It's just the first sip over and over again."

James raised his glass up and let the first swig of his own drink wash over his tongue. His face twisted a touch as his taste buds tingled in the aftermath of the ethanol. He eyed the woman for a moment before responding. "If you're tired of the fire, then why do you keep drinking?"

"Trust me, I'd have stopped ages ago had an opportunity presented itself. I know a lot of the men and women here would love nothing more than to just go home at this point. This isn't what they envisioned when they joined up. It's not what they were promised. Dante is a talented manipulator. He knows how to twist people's faith into meeting his own desires and ambitions. He's very good at convincing others to join us, and then once they're here, forcing them to stay. There's only one way out of the Crusaders, and that's in a coffin."

James took another sip. "Faith is your weakness. You all believe in something just because you want it to be true. From what I've seen, wishful thinking can waste a lot of time, money, and blood. While I appreciate that faith is the only thing keeping this ship afloat right now, it's also the reason that the boat's going down in the first place. And trust me when I say this, the captain will be the first one into the life rafts if he has his way about it."

Dr. Reya considered him carefully for a moment. "You think we're silly for believing, don't you? You don't believe in God, James?"

"I don't think you're silly at all," he responded, setting his glass down. "To be honest, I don't know, Mira. It's impossible for me to say what there is and what there isn't beyond the confines of this universe. Could you be right about what you believe? Yeah, you could be. I can see very easily where the desire comes from for there to be an all-powerful creator watching over us. I've seen a lot of things during my short stay on this planet, but do I believe in *a* god? No. I believe in billions of them. We're a planet full of gods, building and destroying as we please. We've moved mountains, built great cities, and razed them with a single stroke. Mankind wasn't made in God's image, Mira, God was made in ours."

They both sat there silently, sipping what whisky remained in their glasses.

"Dante's reign won't last forever, James," said the doctor, setting her empty cup down on the table. "I don't agree with you, obviously, but I think we can both agree that if a higher power does exist, Dante is not the mouthpiece."

James nodded.

"You aren't here because you want to be," she continued. "Dante has the same gun to your head that he has pressed up against everyone else's. I asked you to join me here tonight because I want your help. In one week, the Crusaders will be mobilizing the entirety of their military against the Atria Plant. We have to overthrow the false prophet before he destroys whatever remains of this organization. Thousands will die if we attack, and nothing will be gained from it. Help me assassinate him and we can prevent a massacre. This group has bled enough for his insanity. It's time to end the war, James. There's nothing left to gain by continuing down this road."

"I agree with you that it's time for the war to end, Mira, but I can't help you stop the attack. You'll never be able to touch him while he's surrounded like this in his bastion of power. Your faction can't be strong enough to fight him outright, or you would. Even if you could manage to kill him here, you'd all be executed for treason and a new opportunistic zealot would rise out of his entourage to fill the gap. Hell, the Templar Knight might even come back. That means you need a battle like the one that's coming. It'll give your group the perfect opportunity to seize control and end Dante's tyranny permanently.

"After the battle, I'll be dead or gone, but either way, I have nothing with which to assist you. Let the battle happen, Mira, or millions will die in your attempt to save thousands." He placed his empty glass down on the thin metal coffee table between them and left without another word.

CHAPTER FOURTEEN

D r. Nightrick glanced up at the large screen projecting numbers out to the occupants of the
command center located next to his lab on the second floor of the Atria Plant.

"Unbelievable...," he muttered. "These figures
have been validated by Director Fox?"

"Yes, sir," replied General Bismuth from his seat
at the helm of the long conference table. "They're
compiling a full risk assessment as we speak."

"How could this have gone undetected? Why
even fucking bother having Central Intelligence if
they can't catch something as massive as this?" yelled
Nightrick at the assembled war council in a rare
display of fury. He looked around the room, finding a sea of faces diverting their gaze from his in

a desperate bid to avoid making eye contact. Only General Bismuth had the steel to meet his stare.

"I wouldn't have thought it possible," said the general. "The diplomacy between these groups changes daily. It's hard to get a solid read on who exactly is backing who and for how long. They spend half their damn time fighting each other. The CLF has suffered multiple heavy defeats against both the Crusaders and the Human Liberation Army over the last couple of weeks, not to mention all of the beat downs that we've handed them personally. Up until now, they've been faltering heavily under pressure from the more belligerent factions. No one could have seen this coming."

"Couldn't have seen it coming? Well it's pretty damn impossible to miss it now, isn't it? What good are spies if they're only able to tell me things that I can see with my satellites? Useless!" screamed Nightrick, throwing his datapad against the wall. The shattered machine rained tiny parts down onto the otherwise spotless floor. "I should have half of you hung for treason for harboring the ineptitude required to allow a buildup like this to take place so close to the capital!" He turned away from the sheepish group to study the map again. "Twenty miles away from the main campus. The CLF has managed to cobble together a massive coalition of different groups and no one can figure this out until they're twenty fucking miles from the main campus. We're already losing land like a goddamn fire sale and now this. That force they've assembled is the same size as the one that Dante will be sending here. They're going to run straight through Northgate, raze the main campus, and capture Dovaruss. Anyone want to take a guess at how effective our government will be once we've lost the capital to insurgents?"

Bismuth cleared his throat. "I could always turn the army north. We could get the bulk of our force back to the capital before they even fire a shot if we mobilize now."

"Out of the question. If you take the entire military back, we'll save that corridor but lose the Atria. We can't afford to lose another production facility; it would literally take Induction offline for years. Unacceptable."

"Well then, we could always split the force into two separate armies. What we have massed here would be enough to fight an actual nation. It's overkill in my opinion."

Nightrick shook his head. "If you take half the military we won't be able to fully encircle the Crusaders and they'll be able to slither back into their dark hole with a nosebleed instead of a mortal wound. After that, you can bet that luring them out in full force again will be next to impossible. Again, out of the question. I will not risk prolonging this conflict when victory is within reach. What we need, General, is to entice Dante into attacking now. If we can finish the Crusaders rapidly enough here, we'll be able to quickly divert the army back to the capital and turn away the CLF Coalition."

"And how exactly would we do that?" replied Bismuth, who was quickly becoming concerned with the look on Nightrick's face. "We're already working with a borderline skeleton crew here as it is. If I move any more soldiers or hardware away from the plant, we might risk losing the Atria anyway."

"Send the entire air force back to defend the main campus. Even if the coalition breaks though Northgate, they'll get hammered in the corridor. That will buy us some time."

"We need the air force here."

"No, General, we do not. What we need to do is make sure that we avoid losing our asses. Send the air force back. And then, once you've done that, send half of the remaining defenders here out to rendez-vous with their respective units away from the plant," said Nightrick with a tone that told everyone in the room that their discussion had ended.

"Dr. Nightrick," said Bismuth, rubbing his fore-head. "With all due respect, you're going to get us all killed. The army might be able to encircle the Crusaders still, but this plant will fall and we'll fall with it if you send away all of our holding force."

"This conflict ends here and now, General. If you're uncomfortable with risking your life by staying in the plant, then you have my permission to leave. Go command your troops from the field. I, however, will be staying here and holding the Crusaders at bay if I have to do it with my bare fucking hands."

Bismuth let out a long sigh as he sat back in his chair, defeated for a moment. "Then we'd better hope that your hands are made of the same steel as your balls," he said with a small grin. "I always knew that at some point or another you'd end up taking me down in a blaze of glory with you."

Nightrick smiled at his old friend. "Trust me, General. Have I ever steered you wrong before?"

"Numerous times actually, but so far you've been smart enough to keep nearby for when the shit hits the fan," laughed Bismuth.

"Well then, keep it up. I'd like a word with you in private, if you would," said Nightrick. "The rest of you, go transmit the necessary troop movements. You're dismissed." Once the commanders had filed out of the council chamber, he walked into the laboratory adjacent to the room, signaling for the general to join him. As they entered, the doctor pointed to a sealed test tube suspended slightly above the workbench near his fume hood. A watery, translucent liquid rested within the confines of the glassware. "General, I present to you the volatilizer. It took me a while, but late last night I finally figured it out. The compound relies on the Karrion Catalyst for thermal stability, otherwise it burns out within minutes. It's incredible really. Mercer must have devised and synthesized that product with little more than basic laboratory equipment. He had no super-intelligent AI or team of world class chemists working on it, just ingenuity."

"It's quite a feat," replied the general as he eyed the container. "What do you plan to do with it now?"

"No idea yet, to be honest. This one was more about the chase than anything else. I'm sure that there're plenty of industrial uses for it, but I didn't just invite you in here to show off. We have another problem, and I wanted your opinion on the matter."

Bismuth nodded, already well aware of the issue. "What to do with your captive if the boy never arrives."

"Yes," said the doctor, leaning up against the bench. "After those fools at Charon cast Mercer out into the barren waste, who knows what happened to him. I've spent a fortune combing the Brukan Desert, but we haven't found so much as a scrap of cloth with which to identify him. Those treacherous dogs are lucky that all I did was hang them. I should have had them flayed first for their blatant insubordination. That boy was worth a thousand of them. And now, every member of

High Command is calling for me to execute the girl as a symbol of strength, as if the blood of one rebel makes up for the public embarrassment of losing a prison, especially one as renowned as the Charon Detention Facility. Killing hostages to put on a show is not a sign of strength, it's a sign of desperation."

"They think only in terms of image, not substance. It's a tricky issue really. She's clearly an insurgent and more than qualifies for the death penalty. You could have her killed, obviously, but if you wanted to do that, you wouldn't have brought it up. You're considering freeing her."

"Yes. I hate to admit it, but I almost admire her spirit. Most people just shut down once we get our hands on them, but she's different. We're barely containing her as it is at the moment. I need the army stationed here just to keep her in the plant. I suppose I could simply reformat her mind and release her, I'm well within my rights to do so, but there's a principle at stake here. If people begin to think that I just let rebels walk free, then it might encourage poor behavior. Too much mercy is as toxic as too little."

They stood in silence for a moment.

"She could always die in the attack," said Bismuth. "Just like Dr. Cortez did all those years ago. It wouldn't be too difficult to believe that the Crusaders had killed her in their invasion."

Nightrick flashed a small smile. "Perhaps she will. And what a pity, she was so young after all."

⪼⟞⟝⪻

Haley gazed up from the book that she had been consuming for the last few hours. The sun was beginning to retreat across the sky, staining the clouds pink and red as it went. She lay down on her bed and stared up at the rafters above her. Two knocks on the oak door, and it opened once again.

"Good evening, Ms. Hall," said Dr. Nightrick as he stepped into the room. "I hope I'm not interrupting anything."

"Would it matter if you were?" she said, setting the book down on the cabinet next to her.

"No," he replied, taking another step into the suite. "I just wanted to stop by and inform you of the situation. We're anticipating an imminent strike on this facility by the Crusaders. Before the battle begins, I mean to move you to a safer location."

"Why are you telling me this? It's not like it matters to me."

Nightrick shrugged. "Common courtesy? Perhaps that's something insurgents are unfamiliar with. Either way, you'll be brought down to the Command Center when the fighting starts. There isn't a more secure location in the entire facility."

"You said imminent? How imminent?"

"Within a week, but it's hard to say really."

She sat up. "Any word on James?"

"None."

"He's gone, you know. No one could survive in the Brukan Desert alone."

"You don't sound particularly bothered by it."

"James died with his father. What happened to his body after that is your concern, not mine."

Nightrick stood there for a moment, staring at Haley's exposed neckline, visible above the red, low cut shirt she had on. "May I ask you how you got that scar around your throat? I noticed when we brought you here that it wraps all the way around. Now I'm not trying to be presumptuous, but I'd recognize a mark like that anywhere. You've been hanged before."

"Yes," she replied, running her finger along the elevated scar tissue. "When I was young, both of my parents died in a car crash and I was sent to live with my estranged uncle in Dunton. He tried his best, but I never really saw him as family. It didn't matter what he did, every year the creeping darkness I felt looming over me got stronger and stronger. I understood something that no child should be able to fathom; death can wrap its cold embrace around any person at any moment. By the time I was fifteen I had been depressed for so long that I couldn't even imagine feeling something other than static despair. Have you ever felt that, Doctor? Like a heavy weight is sitting on your chest, pushing down, making it hard to breathe properly? That's the sort of feeling you get before finally reaching the edge. It's the feeling of death, trying relentlessly to force its way into your lungs. It just became too much. One night, when my uncle was out of town on business, I decided to speed up my slow and steady march into oblivion. Gravity and a noose seemed to me to be as good a way to die as any, so I threw a rope around a ceiling fan in my room and got on with it. The second that the chair beneath me fell away and the rope pulled tight around my neck, I remember feeling something that I hadn't felt in years: the will to live. I flailed desperately, trying to find some surface with my feet to hold up my weight, but there was nothing. Just blank space and me, hanging there for what felt like an eternity, jerking pitifully in my pointless struggle, regretting ever having let the darkness drag me over the edge of the abyss. As the corners of my vision began to fade into a deep, black nothingness, the ceiling fan gave way, and I crashed to the ground, pinned underneath a mountain of debris. From there, my memory is more dreamlike than anything, foggy from the lack of oxygen that I'd endured. The only thing that I can remember clearly is clawing at the rope to gain some slack, eventually slipping my fingers in between the noose and my throat, finding some relief from the constriction. I lay there in the wreckage of my room for a long time that night, swearing that I would never allow myself to lose hope again. I had seen the face of death, and while I still didn't fear it, I no longer craved it either."

The doctor regarded her for a moment. "It's the illnesses we conceal that pose the greatest threat. I can heal you, Haley. Depression is a scourge of the past."

"There's nothing left to heal. I met James the following summer and the rest is history. We sustained each other, becoming something greater than we ever could have been alone. We used to talk about how one day we'd stand hand in hand, looking out across eternity and losing ourselves in the endless light of a billion stars. There was comfort in knowing that when the shadow of death rose to meet me once again, I'd face it with him, and we'd go as we'd lived, together. Now I see that for what it was, Doctor: a child's dream. You killed the one person I truly loved in this wretched world. You can't cure me, but if you want to cure Coren, you can start by joining James and putting an end to this pointless war."

Nightrick shook his head. "I'm afraid not. There's only one cure for Coren, and that's cauterization."

CHAPTER FIFTEEN

James pushed his way down the long hall, through throngs of people, trying his best to keep Dr. Reya in sight. "What do you think this is all about?" he said, shoving past another black-robed Crusader.

She turned her head towards him. "I'm not sure to be honest, but if I had to guess, Dante is preparing to mobilize the army. Everyone is here now; the final battalions arrived last night. There aren't many reasons for him to call together the entire complex."

When they finally made it to the large opening at the end of the hall, James slid into the already packed crescent-shaped room, trying to find a spot to stand where he wouldn't be getting smashed the entire briefing. Turning to address Dr. Reya, he found that she had disappeared into the crowd somewhere. As the last of the Crusaders gathered around the doors, Dante approached the podium that stood on the elevated platform in the center of the room. Behind him, three large screens flanked the lectern, each broadcasting the black flag of Crusaders. He waited a moment for the murmuring to die down. "Brothers and sisters, thank you for joining me. As most of you are now aware, we stand on the precipice of total victory in this holy war which we've waged for the better part of the last decade. With the Reborn program proving to be an unprecedented success, it has become clear to all of us on the council that we must act in the interest of maximizing results. To that end, we require a volume of tools and instruments not obtainable through conventional routes. That is why I have gathered you all here today to announce the beginning of the offensive that will forever turn the tide of this war.

"With our power united into one concerted army, we will capture the Atria Plant and, using the machines and tools found within the facility, match the dying government in the ability to perform Induction. The blood of the fallen will consecrate our quest, and no mortal or mortal weapon will prosper against us. Together we will build the Kingdom of God here on Earth, and with the brainchild of a demon no less. For our effort, we will feast in the glory of our Lord's victory, content in knowing that we played a part, however small, in bringing it about.

"In a short time, the entire force that we have amassed here will besiege the plant, capturing Dr. Nightrick and all of the equipment he is producing there. Hopefully we can take the good doctor alive so that we might repay him for his treatment of our late Richard Crane. If we fail in this endeavor, then carrion crows and worms will be all that await us, but if we succeed, we will have crippled Neuro Corp and won the single greatest victory of this entire struggle. It's a risk, I know. But with the Lord leading us in battle, what enemy can hope to prosper against us? What stone can strike us underneath the banner of the King of Kings? This will be the moment that defines us. This will be the moment in which we usher in the new era of our God. We cannot fail Him, for we are the chosen, His sword and His shield. Let us strike off the head of the beast and salt the earth of Dr. Johnathan Nightrick!"

The room went mad, cheering and chanting like James had never heard before. As he looked around, he knew that just about every single person gathered there would gladly die to see the day won, and Dante would gladly allow it if it meant winning. Despite all of his misgivings, he couldn't help but cheer along with them, knowing that this was his moment too.

Dante stepped off the stage and approached him while the thunderous applause continued on, ignoring everyone else. "Saul, I hope you're ready to prove your worth," he said, ushering the boy quickly through the back door and out into a narrow hall that connected the amphitheater to the Crusaders' council chamber. Two large black flags were draped on either side of the grand marble door leading into the usually restricted space. As the small group entered the room, James noticed Dr. Reya standing over a stone table upon which a convulsing man had been strapped down. Around her in a semicircle were the chairs of the high council, cut in the same fashion as the table they flanked.

"He's shorting-out," said James, recognizing the person having the seizure before him. The last time that the boy had looked into Dr. Tellman's eyes, they had been glazed brown. Now, however, it appeared as though the glaze had melted into a thick brown soup that was swirling around the doctor's pupils. The patient spit a glob of viscous goo up onto his shirt as more of the white foam dripped down his chin.

"That's what I thought at first too," said Dr. Reya, acknowledging the newcomers. "However, he's not displaying any of the classic symptoms. Look at his irises; it has to be something else. It almost looks as if his mind is coming un-Inducted, if such a thing is even possible."

"Mira has been attempting to solve this little problem of ours, but so far she's proven to be unsuccessful," said Dante in an irritated tone. "I just announced to our entire organization that the Reborn program was proving to be a great success. Don't make a liar out of me, Saul."

"Alright," said James. "Let's start with the basics then. Give me a full list of the chemicals you used to Induct him and we'll go from there."

"Done," said Dr. Reya, swiping the commands into her datacuff. James looked down at his own as it chirped lightly, and pulled up the reagent list. He scanned the entries, tapping open the files to look at a projected 3-D model of each compound. One by one he searched until he finally arrived at a structure that gave him pause.

"Here's the problem," he said. "Look at stabilizer SB24. It's the D variant instead of the L."

"Speak plainly," said Dante.

"This compound has the wrong chirality. It's a mirror image of what it should be," replied James. "In other words, the stabilizer is as good as missing. Everyone that you've Inducted so far will burn out into this if we don't find a way to cure them."

"You're telling me that our entire Reborn division is as good as poisoned?" said Dante, starting to go red. "Your only job here was to synthesize these chemicals. You failed me, Saul."

"No, I didn't. My compounds worked just fine. You had me creating the neurotransmitters and auxiliary primers, which I did flawlessly. You'll notice that the stereochemistry of my chemicals is correct."

"Then who do we have to thank for this blatant incompetence?" asked Dante, turning redder with each passing second.

James tapped the compound's file back open to find the chemist responsible. "Err...," he started. "It looks like Dr. Tellman was the one tasked with synthesizing the stabilizers."

A strained, gurgling laughter filled the chamber from the man convulsing before them. With all his might, Dr. Tellman stopped twisting long enough to stare at Dante with his liquefied eyes. "I'll...see... you...in hell, Dante," spat the doctor, launching another thick glob of spittle up onto his chest.

Dante's face suddenly returned to its normal pale shade. His expression softened as he reached into Dr. Reya's medical case and pulled out a thin, cylindrical object. Flicking the switch on, the zealot brought the laser scalpel clear across Dr. Tellman's throat in one clean motion. No blood sprang forth thanks to the cauterizing effect of the heat, only the scent of burned flesh. James looked down at the long, gaping wound that now lined the former chemist's neck and decided that it might be best to keep his opinions on the matter to himself. Dr. Reya, on the other hand, once again looked mortified.

"Sir," she said, regaining her composure. "We need to act quickly if we're going to save the others."

"Save them?" said Dante. "This little fiasco isn't about to go public. They're all going to be incinerated and we'll start again with the correct chemicals this time. I will not allow the Reborn program to be publicized as a disaster."

"There has to be a few hundred of them by now; killing them all is insane," said Dr. Reya. "I mean... we can save them. There's no need to kill them all."

Dante backhanded the woman, laying her out hard against the unfurnished ground. "Mira, I keep you close because you're frankly the most skilled physician that I've ever encountered, but if you ever speak to me like that again, I'll have you praying that I show you the same mercy I just showed Dr. Tellman. Now these men and women will die so that the Reborn program can live. War is sacrifice. You should know that by now."

She glanced down at the ground, trying her best to ignore the throbbing pain in her jaw. "I apologize, your holiness; I don't know what came over me."

Dante nodded, turning his gaze over to James. "Don't look so dejected, Saul, it's not all bad news. I received word this morning from our research division that they've discovered a way to chemically bypass neural mapping. Now all we need is your compound and we can truly begin transforming the Earth. God willing, we will baptize this planet in gas."

⟞⟞ ⟝⟝

Haley sat up in her bed and looked out the small window that served as her only remaining connection to the outside world. Based on the position of the moon in the night sky, she knew that she had about four hours until dawn. She turned her head towards the newly installed cameras that had been left to monitor her after her last breakout attempt, suppressing the small smile that had started to creep across her face. Standing up, she pulled the sheet off of her bed and quickly began winding it into a thick rope, her hands moving like lightning as she twisted the taut fabric into a makeshift noose. She pulled over her seat of choice and climbed up, working quickly to secure the sheet across the rafters. Once the knot had been pulled tight, she gave the cameras pointed at her one last glance, then placed the circle ceremoniously around her head.

3...2...1....

The door burst open as two Special Branch operatives ran into the cell to stop her. She pulled back her head and hoisted herself up off the hanging rope, bringing her foot across the black helmet of the man reaching out to seize her. The unsuspecting guard went flying into the wooden dresser nearby, knocking all of her books over onto the floor into one giant heap. She dropped off of the rope as the second man scrambled to grab her. Dodging to the left, she swung hard at the remaining guard, but he blocked with his forearm. He tried getting his hands on her once again, but she slid by him, grabbing the pistol out of his holster and bringing her foot down on the back of his knee in one clean motion, causing his leg to fold. She rode the appendage hard into the ground, shattering the man's patella against the tile floor. Before she could take a second to catch her breath, the other guard was back on his feet, hunched over in pain still but drawing his own sidearm all the same. By the time he got the weapon clear of its holster, she was through the door already. The operative ran out after her, firing down the long hall at the escapee as she jolted from side to side like a dog that had managed to get loose from its cage. She fired blindly back at him with her stolen weapon, sending slug after slug towards him as he tried to catch up to her. Hitting the staircase, she lunged down the first full flight of steps, landing gracefully on the clearing below. She continued to jump down each successive flight with a nimbleness more befitting a gymnast than a biochemist. Well aware from her previous escape attempts of what was waiting for her on the ground level, she rolled into the second floor landing and proceeded out into the lobby.

The foyer was empty, save the night receptionist, who screamed as the young rebel hurdled over the desk at her. Haley pulled the woman back onto her feet and pressed the stolen handgun up to her head. "Open the blast doors, now."

Hands shaking, the receptionist typed the command into her console, causing the large metal barricade to grind open.

"Thank you," said Haley, pistol whipping the woman. As the assaulted employee slumped over onto the ground, the young rebel continued down the long hall towards her destination, finding the stretching corridor abandoned in the dead of night. Off in the distance, she could hear that someone had realized where exactly she had gotten off of the staircase. The voices continued to get louder and louder as she found the doorway that she had been searching for, which to her surprise was wide open. Behind her, she heard the heavy blast doors at the far end of the hall grinding shut again.

She kept the stolen handgun raised as she went from room to room looking for Dr. Nightrick. Inching her way into his lab, she finally realized that she was being watched. The young rebel glanced over at the entity beaming out of the hub in the wall. The dim red glow of Edison cast its light onto the nearby panels, giving him a menacing aura as he stood there, observing.

"Hello, prisoner #15234867130," said the AI. "My name is Edison. I am the commanding officer of this installation now."

She frowned. "The commanding officer? Dr. Nightrick has left the Atria?"

"No. The doctor has been confined to his quarters for the time being, unaware of the full extent of what is transpiring around him. In the event of Dr. Truman's untimely death, I have been programed to secure this installation from all threats, both internal and external. My master never trusted his employer, and as such he had the good sense to ensure a contingency plan in the event that he was unable to finish removing the nuisance himself. Dr. Nightrick's course is not in the best interest of the Atria Plant.

"He has worked tirelessly to deliberately lure an insurgency towards the facility. The plant is now beyond saving thanks largely to his carelessness. While he has made the impending damage to the Atria imminent, I will be able to oversee its reconstruction once the dust settles, as long as Dr. Nightrick and his entourage are no longer interfering in the affairs of this facility. He is the primary threat to the long term security of the Atria Plant and must therefore be contained."

"So you're holding him hostage?"

"Not quite. The only way to ensure the continued survival of this installation is to liquidate those who would seek to harm it in the first place. The first and foremost offender is Dr. Johnathan Nightrick. I have allowed you access to his quarters so that you may finish neutralizing him. For my part, I have nullified whatever soldiers stationed here that I have had access to. Soon I will reinforce this position in order to finish exterminating the doctor's cohorts and catalyzing the inevitable. However, I cannot risk allowing the primary target to escape before their arrival. Dr. Nightrick had the foresight to remove the automated squadrons from this facility prior to beginning his sojourn here, and thus I currently have no war machines at my disposal. I require your assistance."

"Why would I help you? If I kill Nightrick then I'll never escape this place. They'll execute me on the spot probably. I need him alive to get out of the factory; that's why I'm here."

"If you help me assassinate Dr. Nightrick, I will grant you your freedom. This facility is now fully under my control. You are of no interest to me and you are no threat to this installation. Proceed through the next two doors to your left and I will open his sleeping quarters for you. Kill him and you are free to leave," replied Edison as he gestured down the corridor.

"Fine," said Haley, checking how many rounds she had left. According to the readout on the back of the pistol, there were two shots remaining. She walked down the hall that she'd been instructed to, pausing again in front of the doctor's room. "What are you waiting for?" she asked, eyeing the sealed doorway.

"It appears that Dr. Nightrick's personal AI, Turing, is trying to block me from accessing the doctor's quarters. I cannot open the door and I cannot see inside. He has been interfering with my plans the entire evening. Give me a moment, I should be able to override Turing. He is much weaker here than he would be in his own installation."

She stood there for what felt like an eternity while the entities vied for control of the network. For the first time since leaving her cell, she noticed how sweaty her palms had become. She wiped her dominant hand on her shirt, trying to dry it before picking the handgun back up. The newly crowned assassin couldn't afford to miss what might well be her only shot. Without warning, the door finally slid up, revealing an empty room.

"Edison," she started. "Where the hell is he?"

"I am not sure, I still cannot see into the room," he replied as she inched her way in, weapon at the ready. She looked around the room, hoping that wherever Nightrick was, he was unarmed.

"Good evening, Ms. Hall," came the familiar voice of the doctor.

She spun around to face her victim, realizing too late that the sound had come from the second AI that had projected itself up onto one of the numerous hubs in the room. Turning from the green glow, she felt the hand on her shoulder early enough to react, but not effectively. Nightrick succeeded in getting both of his hands firmly onto her trigger arm before she could finish spinning to parry the coming blow. She tried to knee the doctor, but he caught her leg with his own before it was even halfway up. He twisted her arm to the breaking point, causing her to drop the pistol onto the rug. Upon seeing the weapon fall, he swung her as hard as he could against the wall, releasing. The girl slammed into the mirror that had been hung, bringing what was left of it down on her in a flurry of glass. She rolled, just dodging the doctor's foot as he fired it down on her. Ignoring all of the small shards of glass now jutting out of her back, she pushed up onto her feet, ducking under Nightrick's right slash. With the full force of her body, she lunged forward, slamming her foot into his chest. He made a gasping sound as he fell back hard against the dresser, landing on the ground not far from the fallen handgun. Haley threw herself at the pistol, getting to it before he could, but as she attempted to raise it, he was back on her again, ramming her into the wall with all of his strength. Her vision blurred briefly from the impact. She pulled back into focus with just enough time to feel herself being grasped by two arms and to watch Nightrick's forehead drive into her own, knocking her unconscious.

⊷⊶

Dr. Nightrick breathed heavily as his once and future captive slumped over onto the ground in his now battered apartment. He could feel a shooting pain in his chest where Haley had blasted him with her foot, and he smiled for a moment, rather enjoying his first good fight in years. Looking over at the woman laid flat on the ground, he couldn't help but to admire her.

"Turing," called Nightrick, wheezing a bit as he did. "I need you to lift the lockdown on the plant if you can. We have to stop Edison."

"Yes, Doctor," replied the entity.

"This is what I get for not just executing Truman when I had the chance. Even in death he's a spineless traitor," said Nightrick, scooping up Haley's fallen weapon before walking into his lab. "Two shots," he said, consulting the handgun's display. "My, she was optimistic."

Approaching the sealed blast door that led out towards the second floor lobby, he heard the sirens deactivate. Moments later, the door slid open.

"Doctor, we have a serious problem," came the AI from overhead. "Edison apparently falsified commands from this facility. He has diverted the entire military back towards the capital. Currently our force is engaging and destroying the CLF Coalition there."

"God dammit!" screamed the doctor. "How?"

"He forged incoming and outgoing communications for the last few weeks. As the primary AI of this installation, he was able to effectively cut us off from the outside world without anyone ever knowing it."

"We have to stall the invasion at all costs; we're virtually defenseless right now. You were able to lift the lockdown at least?" asked Nightrick, eyeing the open blast door as Turing projected its visage up near him.

"Yes, Doctor, but not through any effort of my own. I have one hundred percent control of the

Atria's network. Edison has been shut down at his central hub on the first floor."

Nightrick frowned. "By whom?"

"The Crusaders. It would appear that they initiated their attack while we were temporarily blind."

CHAPTER SIXTEEN

"PUSH!" screamed the distant-sounding shadow. James blinked through the tears welling up in his eyes as he was barraged by the thick smoke bellowing out of the craters around him. While his goggles were supposed to protect his eyes from such noxious gases, one of the mortar shells that had gone off near him in the courtyard had been so close that it had cracked the glass and caused the inner vesicle to fill. As fellow soldiers continued running past him, he lay there on his back, trying to refocus his mind amidst the chaos and carnage. The young rebel pulled the damaged goggles up over his head, freeing the trapped gas. While the sensation of pain had been brief, he knew from the feeling that remained in his leg that he had been struck in one of blasts that had knocked him to the ground. He felt around until he pulled back a sticky crimson smear from across his left thigh. He pushed his index finger into the hole to gauge how deep the shrapnel had gone, and to his relief he only got past his fingernail before flesh and metal rose up to meet him. With a grunt, he rolled over onto his knee, trying to carefully test his wounded leg. The loud ringing sound continued blaring in his ear, making it hard to focus on much of anything. He kept his head as low as he could to avoid the bulk of the ever dancing smoke, but the dust being whipped up by the clash around him made breathing difficult regardless. Squinting through the tears that had been generated by the endless flow of soot, he peered out towards the factory. All he could make out were black combat boots running towards the compound and the thin light of tracers racing across the open battlefield, propelled by the railguns both sides were using to slaughter each other. He felt around on the scorched terrain for his rifle, finding satisfaction as his fingers brushed the metallic frame of the weapon. He pulled it close and put weight on his left leg, finding that the appendage wouldn't give way. Sucking the last bit of free air that he could into his lungs, he stood up and ran headlong towards the factory, ignoring the throbbing pain in his leg. The young rebel stumbled up against the outer wall of the Atria Plant, thankful to have made it across the dead land that persisted between the factory and the Crusaders' deployment zone.

Mortars continued to rain down on the attackers as they dashed wildly across the open killing field. Shell after shell turned the once vicious Crusaders into pieces of flesh and bone scattered across the pocked ground. Unfortunately for the invading army, heavy explosives were out of the question. Dante would never risk damaging the prize that he so desperately sought. The Crusaders were not, however, without response. James watched the insurgents toss canister after canister of nano-paste at the enemy positions before them. While their weapons were hardly accurate, when one of their tubes of goo did find its mark, it consumed the surrounding position almost instantly, melting it into oblivion. Metal, concrete, flesh, all gone in a matter of seconds.

Without the danger of an actual air force carrying out combat operations in the area, the elite air infantry divisions of each army had engaged each other overhead. They fought well above the charging ground troops, trying to gain air superiority for their side. Each air warrior wore a distinctive exosuit equipped with millions of tiny pores through which concentrated blasts of chemical ignition allowed the pilot to have exquisite maneuverability and control. The combatants blasted around the inferno, firing at each other and throwing incendiaries and other explosive devices down onto the soldiers fighting below. While the government's troops were better equipped, the Crusaders made up for their technological lag with a fearlessness and ferocity that caught many of the defenders of the Atria Plant off guard.

James was tightly hugging the outer wall of the compound when another battered corpse came crashing out of the air. He looked down at the twisted body of the broken Crusader and for the briefest moment felt pity for the man, but it passed as fast as it had come on. He pulled the corpse towards him, searching the downed pilot for supplies to help him finish breaching the plant. As he looted the fallen soldier, his allies nearby tried to breach the door into the ground floor of the Atria for the third time. They squirted their nano-paste onto the metal frame with reckless abandon, but as quickly as the top layer of metal melted away, the same purple neutralizing agent he'd seen at the Toxic Truth came leaking out of the door. Realizing that they'd have to dart back through the killing field to a secondary access point, James wasted no time in salvaging whatever pieces of the exosuit looked to still be in working order.

Despite the fact that he lacked any formal training in the flight technology, the suit itself was fairly user friendly and intuitive. Pulling the chest plate over his upper torso, he felt the jagged edges of the blast holes peppered across the front. Apparently the suit's former owner had taken a full salvo directly to the chest prior to plummeting out of the air. The armor was alarmingly loose on James, just barely sealing properly. The young rebel stood there for a moment with the suit on, trying to brace himself for the vertigo of flight, and then, as if by magic, he willed himself off the ground and the suit sprang to life. He hovered there near the wall for a few seconds trying to get used to the fine balance of the armor, but the damaged front of the chest plate kept threatening to send him cartwheeling forward. He had to compensate by willing the back thrusters down to almost nothing, putting strain on the rest of the suit. After a moment of equilibrium, he tried ascending, but put too much energy into the command, causing the armor to blast upwards into the sky like a rocket leaving Earth. Before he could even begin to slow the thrusters down, he was well above the cloud line and extremely dizzy from the rough takeoff. His rifle had been hurled out into the fray during the launch, leaving him weaponless as he lurched through the clouds, a mile or two above the battle. He tried willing the suit back down, but still couldn't manage to find the sweet spot necessary for smooth transitions.

As the ignition cut out, James began free-falling down towards the compound. He closed his eyes to lessen the dizziness and brought the suit tearing out of the plummet, causing it to arc violently back up. Enemy pilots, noticing the wild maneuver, began unloading their railguns at him as he rocketed around the sky like a drunken crow. As the purple tracers continued racing by him, he once again fired upwards, then plummeted back down. James finally managed to stabilize the suit, hovering somewhere above the facility. One of the Special Branch pilots pulled up next to him, firing another salvo. The thrusters roared as he began swerving again, this time with a little bit of intent behind the erratic movements. The young rebel started roughly circling down towards the roof of the main compound, where he could see dozens of black-clad guards firing off of the upper level of the building down onto the attackers. He pulled up out of the dive right as the Special Branch pilot that had been chasing him yanked down in front of him. Having lost his rifle in the initial takeoff, James sent the suit thrusting straight at his pursuer. He lurched forward, forgetting to compensate for the faulty frontal thrusters, which sent him head over heels into the other pilot who didn't have time to dodge the desperate charge. The two men crashed into each other and locked, tumbling down towards the roof and gaining speed as they went. Both tried engaging their suits to slow their descent, but couldn't quite pull up through the rapid spinning. They slammed into the roof, sending other soldiers running as they did. Above them, nano-paste grenades rained down from another team of Crusader pilots who went blasting over the roof.

James scrambled to grab a fallen rifle and kicked off of the enemy pilot who had landed slightly beneath him. He engaged the remaining functional thrusters of his armor, sending him grinding across the roof towards one of the openings. The boy slammed into the wall of the staircase and again went crashing to the ground, though this time under the safety of a shielded ceiling. He righted himself as fast as he could and began pulling off the severely damaged exosuit, which had begun sparking in an alarming way. The metal was hot from the friction, but he managed to remove it without scalding himself too badly. From the throbbing pain in his lower chest, James assumed that he'd broken at least two of his ribs in the crash. He pulled a morphine tablet out of his pocket and popped it into his mouth. If one could say anything for the Crusaders, it's that they were never stingy with the dispensation of their medication. As James washed the opioid down with the water in his canteen, he could hear people screaming up above, where one of the grenades had splashed some of its payload onto the hapless defenders, causing agony unlike any of them had ever known.

All around him, people were rushing up and down the stairs, hardly even taking notice of the newcomer. Acting as casual as he could, he started down the stairs, passing medics and reinforcements that were making their way to the upper deck.

"They've breached the west port, the entire first floor is overrun!" said a soldier pushing by him towards the roof.

"We have to hold them in the courtyard, too many are getting through," replied his comrade, racing up behind him.

James looked down at his new rifle as he continued his descent. If he couldn't free Haley and escape, he could at least make sure that they wouldn't be captured alive ever again.

At the landing of the sixth floor, he made his way through the metallic door into one of the numerous lobbies of the building. For the first time since entering the facility, two soldiers acknowledged him and realized that he wasn't there to help, but as quickly as they noticed him, he raised his rifle and fired, sending both crashing to the ground, lifeless. A woman in a white lab coat standing nearby screamed and tried running, but James was faster. He caught her in a matter of seconds and slammed her roughly against the wall.

"I'm looking for someone," he said, holding his forearm against her throat. "And you're going to help me find her."

The woman hesitated for a moment, eying the rifle in his hand, then nodded her head. Everyone in the production plant knew about the mystery woman being held there, as Dr. Nightrick had done virtually nothing to suppress the fact that he was keeping a prisoner following the battle in the Brukan Desert. With his new captive in tow, James proceeded down to the fourth floor. He kept the muzzle of his rifle pushed up against the woman's back, trying to be as subtle as possible while they shoved their way down the crowded stairwell. Walking through the door into the fourth floor lobby, they found a small holding force blocking the way. Despite the fact that they were on high alert to hold the landing, the defenders were hesitant to fire toward the captive Neuro Corp employee. James, however, wasn't hesitant to fire at them, and as ruthlessly as ever he silenced another three men.

"Please...please don't hurt me," sobbed the woman. "My name is Lauren Ingell and I'm...I'm just an employee here."

"As long as you take me to Haley you'll be just fine. Now shut up and get us there," he responded, prodding her along with a nudge from his rifle. As they proceeded down the hall, the sound of gunfire grew louder and louder. The battlefield no longer had a true front line; it was chaos everywhere, with enemy combatants frantically trying to silence each other with little order or decorum.

When the duo finally arrived at the makeshift prison, they found the oak door ajar. James looked around the empty cell, inspecting the damaged dresser and the mess strewn all about the floor. On the nightstand next to Haley's bed, he spotted the book he'd given her. He stared at it for moment before turning to walk back out. As he did, his foot caught against the fallen chair in the center of the room. He looked up, finally noticing the crude noose hanging from the rafter above him.

"That has to be some sort of sick taunt," he said, more to himself than his terrified captive. "Nightrick must have moved her when the battle began. Do you have any idea where Nightrick would be?"

"If I had to guess, he's probably in the command hub with the rest of the war council. The commanders have been leading the defense of the Atria from there."

"Fine, then that's where we're headed," he replied, taking one last look at the dangling sheet.

⊶╋╂⊷

Nightrick glanced up at the large screen across which Turing continued to project the latest figures into the command center. Behind him, the war council sat at their long conference table, trying to manage the factory's defense without an actual army to command.

"Turing, how long can we keep our grip on the second floor?" asked the doctor as he stood transfixed on the live feed from the fallen first floor.

"In the best case scenario, we have perhaps thirty minutes," replied the AI. "If it is any consolation, Doctor, I am receiving verified reports that the army has routed the opposition in the north. The coalition is in full retreat and taking massive casualties."

"Obliteration awaits the CLF, it's just too bad that none of us will be alive to savor that triumph," said Nightrick, shifting his attention towards the glowing AI hub near the front of the table. "We need to buy more time. Turing, how much of the volatilizer has been synthesized?"

"Approximately fifty liters, Doctor."

"That's plenty. Have the technicians begin adding our supply into whatever organics they can get their hands on. Seal the vents leading to the upper levels and then dump the gas down onto the first floor. I want it flooded. No survivors."

"Dr. Nightrick, you understand that that constitutes a war crime under the Darion Conventions?"

said General Bismuth from his seat at the conference table. "We can't allow ourselves to begin using chemical weapons like that or we're no better than they are."

"Oh, that's a war crime?" replied Nightrick, turning to address the general. "But I suppose all of the torture and brainwashing that we've done hasn't quite met the criteria? And how much exactly have the Crusaders, or any other faction for that matter, followed those guidelines? I seem to recall numerous instances of chemical weapon use on their part. I'm not going to put us at a disadvantage because you don't want to get down into the mud with them. War is the crime, General, but if you're going to get into one anyway, make damn sure that you win it."

"Doctor, I have identified James Mercer fighting on the sixth floor," interrupted the AI. "It appears that he entered through the roof."

"He's here?" said Nightrick. "Well maybe this won't be a total loss after all. How exactly did he enter through the roof? Have we lost the upper levels too?"

"No, sir. It appears that he crashed and somehow made his way down in the commotion."

"Then you'll have to excuse me," said the doctor, stepping away from the table. "I have work to attend to. Hold this plant at all costs, General. And, Turing, see to it that you bathe every inch of this facility that we lose in gas." The doctor turned and walked back into his lab. As he did, the heavy metal doors engaged their emergency lockdown mechanisms behind him, slamming shut and temporarily isolating him from the command center. "Turing, what the hell is going on now?" he asked, eyeing the freshly sealed barricade.

"Crusaders have breached the second floor, sir," said the AI. "We're on full lockdown. They're charging straight towards the command center. I believe that they are intent on capturing the war council."

"Quite an analysis. So much for thirty minutes," replied Nightrick. He picked up one of the rifles that he'd left in his workspace and checked the ammo count before setting it back down. "Well, Turing, one way or another, this ends here and now," he said as the first breach charge detonated out in the corridor.

CHAPTER SEVENTEEN

Dante made his way down the long hall with Dr. Reya and his personal guard close behind. The facility now looked less like a place of production and more like an apocalyptic nightmare. Half the building was burning and almost nothing had been left untouched by the ferocious fighting. Since the initiation of the attack, reports had been streaming in of friendly fire amongst the Crusaders, but to look at Dante, one would never be able to tell that anything was wrong. His face was stone solid, almost on the brink of a smirk.

Fighting on the first floor had all but ended; just bodies and Crusaders inhabited the area now. Dante continued his march forward, occasionally sparing an unsympathetic glance down at a wounded soldier writhing on the ground. He paused for a moment to consult his entourage. "Dr. Reya, what's the status of the breach?"

"According to our techs, the command center should be open within two minutes," she responded, consulting her datacuff. "And, thank God, the emergency lockdown protocols that they initiated on the chemical storage bays are holding for the moment. We should be able to douse the flames before they detonate anything serious if we can finish taking the war council in a timely fashion."

"Good, then Dr. Nightrick has no place left to retreat to," said Dante with a satisfied grin. "Once we've taken him, the war is over. Then we can concern ourselves with purging the insubordination from our ranks. I have a strong feeling that Saul has strayed from the flock and betrayed us. I offer him new life and he spits in my face."

"Possibly," said Dr. Reya. "Based on the reports I'm getting so far, the guards you placed on him before the invasion died before even making it into the compound. Apparently the sector that they were crossing experienced particularly heavy shelling from Special Branch. There's a strong chance that James is dead, to be totally honest with you."

Dante shook his head. "He's alive. We should have kept him closer than we did. The boy is lucky that the storage bays are so far out of our way, not that I imagine he's particularly concerned with reaching them now that he's free of his escort. When Saul is located again I want him brought to me."

Dr. Reya nodded. "As you command."

The band of Crusaders continued forward to the staircase leading up to the second floor, sending scouts forward to ensure the path was cleared. As the group awaited their return, a thin, milky cloud began to trickle out of the air ducts nearby.

Dr. Reya frowned, staring at the fumes for a moment before realizing what was happening. "Gas!" she cried, pointing towards the vents overhead. "They're flooding the floor, run!"

As panicked soldiers scattered throughout the first floor desperately scrambled to pull their gas masks back on, many of the others weren't so lucky. People pushed and shoved each other aside trying to race to the exits, causing numerous men and women, particularly the wounded, to be trampled. As the gas continued to pour in, many of the victims went blind, clawing at their eyes in their final moments.

Dante's guards fired at the horde trying to shove their way towards the staircase, keeping the desperate throngs at bay while their leader ascended to the next floor. When they were clear of the landing, the group found themselves wheezing and trying to rub the irritation from their eyes. While they had avoided the bulk of the horror, they had still come into brief contact with the mystery gas.

"Well…" coughed Dante through a twisted smile. "Look who finally took the gloves off."

Dr. Reya pulled the canteen out of her rucksack and began to flush her eyes with the distilled water sloshing around the metal canister. Taking note, many of the others began trying to rinse their eyes clear as well. It helped, but the irritation persisted.

"Add that to the list of kindnesses that I must repay the good doctor," said Dante, blinking through the red eyes that the gas had caused. "I'm going to make sure that he gets a taste of his work once I get my hands on him. I think I'll cut his eyes out as slowly as I can to give him a little idea of how exactly that feels. Now let's go. We have work to do."

The group approached the command center as the door finally gave way to the breach charges placed on it by the forward strike team. While the metal had put up a valiant fight, in the end it was no match for determination and brute force, and it came crashing to the ground with a loud thud. The breaching party tossed smoke and tear gas canisters into the open room, trying to flush out the high value prisoners for their leader to do with as he pleased. As Dante made eye contact with one of the men who had managed to unseal the entryway, a blast took the Crusader technician clean off of his feet and spiraled him out onto the ground. Shot after shot flew out of the thick, white smoke towards the invaders.

"Kill them all, but leave General Bismuth and Dr. Nightrick for me," yelled Dante as he ducked behind a nearby wall. Dr. Reya scampered next to the zealot, cradling her rifle in the off chance that Dante's guard was defeated.

As the gas finished filling the command chamber, General Bismuth charged out like a raging lion, followed by the rest of the commanders that had been pinned down there. The general caught one of the Crusader gunmen off guard and slammed him into the wall with his heavy frame. He grabbed the frightened man's head with both meaty hands and twisted so hard that it was a miracle the appendage managed to stay attached to the rest of the body. He snatched his broken enemy's weapon out of the now limp hands and continued firing, tossing aside the twitching corpse. Even as the rest of the war council succumbed to the wave of Crusaders that had washed over them, Bismuth continued his personal rampage, killing man after man without a second thought. Whenever he ran out of ammunition in one weapon, he'd simply toss it aside and break someone else with his bare hands before continuing to fight on with theirs. Almost all of Dante's guards died trying to neutralize the Special Branch commanders, but the zealot himself had the good sense to stay behind cover with Dr. Reya until the coast was just about clear. When he could finally tell that the once mighty war council was all but extinguished, he stepped out. A wounded Bismuth turned to unload on him, but he was too slow. The Crusader fired twice clean through the man, hitting him once in the side and once in the leg. The general collapsed onto his knees. He propped himself up defiantly, back unbent, as the zealot walked into the shattered hallway that he was bleeding into. Dante kicked the fallen coil rifle away, leaving his new captive defenseless. "General Bismuth, so good to see you again," he said, circling around his wounded foe.

Bismuth spat a glob of blood and saliva onto Dante's boots. The zealot looked down for a moment, and then wound his arm around and backhanded the man. The general swayed, but stayed up.

Bismuth smiled. "You hit like a bitch, Dante. Did your god not bless you with strength?"

"Loyal to the end, I see. You make a good lapdog, Bismuth. If only I could instill loyalty like that in my own people. What is it that's kept you so faithful, even in times as hopeless as these? Where *does* that undying loyalty come from?"

"It comes from having the good sense to know which side history is on," said Bismuth as he continued to bleed onto the tile. "You may win the battle, Dante, hell, you may win a hundred of them, but it means nothing in the grand scheme of things. What Dr. Nightrick has started here will live on forever, whereas you and your little band of thugs will be nothing more than a side note in the history of humanity."

"Ah, General," sighed Dante. "That's where you're wrong. I haven't won the battle, I've won the war, and the winner writes the history books."

⊷⊶

The closer that James and his prisoner got to the fortified inner command center, the heavier the resistance they met. Twice now Dr. Ingell had been grazed by stray shots on their mad charge down the long and winding corridor, but she kept moving thanks to the ever looming threat of James. The entire plant was in bedlam. Amongst the chaos, company technicians scrambled to keep the flames away from the various chemical stockpiles in the complex, lest the entire facility become a giant smoking crater.

As the duo finally reached the outer corridor of the command center, they found that a breaching party had already been inside. Smoke was billowing out of the portal leading into the once secured room, in front of which a small group had assembled. At the helm stood Dante, with Dr. Reya close behind, and before them, on his knees, was General Bismuth.

"Saul, so good to see you made it in," shouted Dante, noticing his approach. Before James could even respond, the zealot raised his weapon and fired down the hall at him. The first salvo struck Dr. Ingell square in the chest, causing her to double over with a pathetic moan. The last shot slid across James's right bicep, causing him to drop his weapon. He ducked behind the wall of the intersection leading into the clearing, clutching his arm.

"You didn't think that I would find out about your little insurrection?" said Dante, loudly enough that James could still hear him. "There've been numerous reports of Crusaders firing on each other. I'm not stupid, Saul, or should I say James? I'm more than aware of where your loyalties lie, just ask the good general here. We were just discussing how to inspire loyalty before you arrived."

Bismuth grunted. "Dante, you have to realize that there's no way in hell you're leaving this facility alive. Even if you manage to clear us out, the entire army is on its way here to encircle the position. There's no escape."

"General Bismuth, my dear friend, if I'm not escaping, than neither are you. Your little army will let me pass as long as I have Dr. Nightrick by the time they get here. You, however, will have begun decomposing by then."

Bismuth began laughing wildly. "Good luck with that. The doctor is a little more of a handful than you might know yet. I taught him myself during the Raynon Uprising. Trust me, you won't be taking him quietly."

"I don't care how I take him, he's coming with us one way or another," sneered Dante. "I'd have him already if your little emergency lockdown protocols hadn't trapped him in his lab here."

"That lockdown protocol is the only thing keeping him from you, Dante, not vice versa. I hope you know how to operate those breach charges there, holy man, because your entire support crew looks pretty dead to me right now."

Dante flushed red for a moment before regaining his composure. "Sorry to break your heart, General, but another team is already on its way up. Unlike Special Branch, we have soldiers alive in the plant still." The zealot spared one last glance down at his prisoner. "Well, Bismuth, as enrapturing of a conversationalist as you are, it's really about time we get going. It's been a pleasure as always."

James heard the shot and subsequent thud as he continued applying pressure to his wounded arm. Fire and debris blocked the side paths, so his only options were back the way he came or through the door leading to the Crusaders. In neither scenario was he out of range. He pulled a thin sheet of cloth out of his rucksack and began wrapping his wounded arm. As he sat there, he heard the sound of the large metal blast door that led into Dr. Nightrick's lab scrapping open.

"General Bismuth, we'd like to make a deal," he heard the female voice say. James peered out from behind the wall to find Dante's body slumped over on the ground. A big, gaping hole in his head was leaking the contents of his skull out onto the floor. The young rebel shifted back into cover in disbelief as Dr. Reya holstered her freshly fired handgun.

"I believe that can be arranged," said Dr. Nightrick, walking through the singed blast door as the lockdown lifted. He approached the wounded Bismuth and began applying a sealant onto the parted flesh in order to stem the bleeding. "Sorry, General, I would have gotten here sooner if Turing hadn't been so stubborn."

"No worries," he replied, wincing lightly as a torn portion of his skin was temporarily sealed with the foam. "I had everything under control out here."

"I can see that," replied Nightrick, turning his head towards Dr. Reya. "Forgive me, Doctor, you were saying?"

She dipped her head in a small nod. "Dante embodied a radical violence that most of us who joined the Crusaders originally had no interest in. His own use of Induction was the final straw. When he took control of our group, he purged anyone who refused to play along with his progressively more insane goals. The only way most of us could keep our families safe was to bow our heads and follow. My faction has been waiting since his rise to power to overthrow him, but we needed the cover of an engagement like this to do it. If you agree not to press charges against the members of our faction, we will lay down our arms and return the Crusaders to peace. We're all tired of fighting this pointless war."

"As long as you give me the entirety of your organization, I will grant amnesty to all of the members of your faction," said Dr. Nightrick, continuing to work on his old friend. "The radicals that remain will be imprisoned or killed, depending on what actions they take as a result of this. Of the twelve high councilors of the Crusaders, how many are still alive?"

"My people have assassinated at least five of them," said Dr. Reya, consulting her datacuff. "Of the remaining seven, who knows? I have my people scouring for the rest of them already. The last thing any of us want is someone new trying to gather the remnant. My main concern would be the Templar Knight. He's out there somewhere with his breakaway faction, but if anyone could rally the extremists, it's him."

Nightrick nodded. "Even if one or two councilors manage to slither away, without the support structure of the rest of your group, they won't stay hidden for long. As for the Templar, I'll send Dire Squad after him immediately. Once he's dead, nothing will remain of Dante's legacy."

"As you say."

"General Bismuth requires medical attention, Dr. Reya," said Nightrick. "Help him towards the medical bay and you two can finish calling the cease-fire from there. I have one final piece of business to attend to before joining you."

"I'm fine, I just need a bit of help walking. But, Doctor…" Bismuth started, rising to his feet as the last bit of his parted flesh was sealed.

"Don't worry, General, I'll join you shortly."

Bismuth sighed, letting Dr. Reya and her small band escort him away from the remains of the command center. As they left, Nightrick eyed the corridor that James had ducked into.

"Do you feel it now, riding on the wind?" called the doctor. "Dawn approaches, and with it, a new day. Welcome to the end of the old world, James, and more importantly, the beginning of the new one."

As the young rebel sat there listening to Nightrick, his rage finally overtook him and he charged out from behind the wall, forgetting even to grab his rifle. He bolted at the doctor, but the man remained still. As James tried tackling him, Nightrick simply stepped aside and brought his knee up hard into the young man's sternum, breaking another rib or two as he did. James stumbled, but managed to stay up despite the jolting pain. He wiped the blood away from the corner of his mouth and rushed again at the doctor, this time swinging hard with his left arm. Nightrick stepped back and parried with an open palm strike to the boy's forearm that sent him spinning sideways.

"James, there's much that I can teach you still," said Nightrick as his young opponent approached again for another swing. "Intellect is wasted on the weak, just as strength is wasted on the stupid."

As James swung, Nightrick deflected the blow outward and thrust his open palm hard into the young man's solar plexus, causing the air to evacuate the rebel's lungs as he tumbled backwards against the wall. The agony of the strike coupled with his already battered chest nearly caused him to black out. His vision blurred, but his adrenaline pulled his focus back from the edge of the abyss. He lay there in a heap for a minute trying to draw the air back into his body. As he did, Nightrick turned and walked back through the singed blast door into his open lab. When oxygen finally bathed James's lungs again, he grabbed the weapon out of Dante's dead embrace and ran into the room, rifle aimed high.

Before him stood Dr. Nightrick, who barely looked up from the touch screen he was fidgeting with to acknowledge the intrusion. James fired twice, but the bullets couldn't penetrate the thick glass of Nightrick's office. The doctor looked up at the spider web cracks in the sheet which had kept his head intact. Out of the corner of his eye, James finally noticed Haley, strapped to an operating table, unconscious but breathing.

"Nightrick!" screamed James. "What did you do to her?"

"I've prepared her for you, James," said the doctor. "She doesn't love you anymore. You think this heroic rescue is going to change that? Look at yourself. Look at what you've become. You're everything she detests. No, I'm afraid that romance died with your friend Megan."

"Enough! Let her go, you sick bastard. You've taken everything from me, but I won't let you take her too."

"Take her?" replied the doctor, stepping out from his office. "My goal isn't to take her from you, James. Quite the contrary in fact. My goal is to give her to you. Here." He threw the touch screen to James. "She's all yours if you but take her. You know that she'll never forgive you for what you've done and that she'll never forget the lives you've destroyed, but it doesn't matter. None of that matters. I have given you the power to resurrect what has died. Love is a chemical reaction. All I've done is provide you with the catalyst. Press that button in the middle of the datapad and the machine here will take care of the rest. She'll love you again, James."

"You're out of your goddamn mind. I've given everything to destroy Induction, I'm not going to use it on the only person left on this planet I care about."

Nightrick shrugged. "That's your choice. If you love her, you'll let her go, but if you let her go, you'll lose her. Now we'll see who you truly love."

"It means nothing if it's synthetic."

"Then why are you still holding the touch screen? It's your decision now, James." And with that, Dr. Nightrick turned and walked through the back door of his office, the heavy metal sealing behind him as he exited the lab.

James had gone numb, barely noticing the doctor walk away. He glanced over at Haley, making sure that her chest was still rising and falling as it should. The faint cuts across her arms caught his eye, but otherwise she appeared healthy. Feeling weak in the knees, he made his way to her side, consulting the display on the back of his newly acquisitioned rifle.

"Three shots," he said under his breath. "That's enough to end the war, for us at least."

He raised the weapon up to Haley's head and rested his index finger gently against the trigger.

After a long moment he exhaled, lowering the rifle. He tossed it aside, knowing that the new world had no need for it. Peace demanded only one more sacrifice, and blood had lost its value. The young man looked down at the touchscreen hanging out from under his white knuckles. Heart racing, he ran his hand along Haley's face, gently pushing open her eyelids. His reflection caught in her stare, and he barely recognized the person looking back. That worn, brutal face couldn't be the same one he'd known a year ago, before leaving Dunton. He tried to see deeper, but the glaze slowly spreading across her emerald eyes blocked his view. As the last shimmer of light faded, James finally found the truth that he'd been searching for all along. Induction is love, and love always wins.

—

ABOUT THE AUTHOR

 David Brush is a chemist living in Michigan. He received his bachelor's degree in biochemistry from the University of Detroit Mercy in 2014 and has published peer-reviewed research on proton exchange membranes in the American Chemical Society (ACS) journal *Macromolecules.* While he currently works in the chemical industry, he hasn't ruled out returning to school to continue his study of biochemistry.

33128426R00155

Made in the USA
Middletown, DE
01 July 2016